THE ONLY SAFE PLACE PLACE LEFT IS THE DARK

WARREN WAGNER

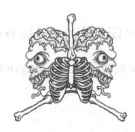

Ghoulish Books
an imprint of Perpetual Motion Machine Publishing
San Antonio, Texas

The Only Safe Place Left is the Dark

ISBN: 978-1-943720-86-6

www.GhoulishBooks.com

Cover by Aidan Mayner

For Aidan

Viruses have no morality, no sense of good and evil, the deserving or the undeserving . . . AIDS is not the swift sword with which the Lord punishes the evil practitioners of male homosexuality and intravenous drug use. It is simply an opportunistic virus that does what it has to do to stay alive.

**—CHRIS CRUTCHER,
King of the Mild Frontier**

Men do not naturally not love. They learn not to.
**—Felix Turner, The Normal Heart
Written by Larry Kramer**

CHAPTER ONE
Silence Equals Life

BY THE SUMMER of 1988, the only thing holding Frankie's bones together was his skin. Those thick, purple lesions were like a kiss of death, and they both had them. Quinton was at least healthy enough to sit at Frankie's bedside, holding his hand and counting his breaths. His mouth and throat were nearly swollen shut from thrush by this point, and his lungs were filled with fluid. Every breath he took felt like an insurmountable task that could very well be his last. It was hard to tell if he knew Quinton was there, or even if he knew what *there* was anymore.

His name was Franklin Jorge Garcia, and within a week he'd be dead. Until then, Quinton remained with him. Those who weren't killed were left waiting. Waiting for a cure. Waiting for the end. They weren't dead yet, but they weren't alive either.

They were zombies.

In the July 3, 1981 edition of the *New York Times*, there was an article on page twenty entitled "RARE CANCER SEEN IN 41 HOMOSEXUALS." In it, columnist Lawrence K. Altman remarked the "cancer is not believed to be contagious, but conditions that might precipitate it, such as particular viruses or environmental factors, might account for an outbreak among a single group."

"The best evidence against contagion," he wrote, "is

I

that no cases have been reported to date outside the homosexual community or in women." This was the first mention of the disease that would eventually be known as HIV/AIDS. It would soon sweep through the gay community and take out anyone it could.

In Vancouver, during the week of July 7, 1996, the theme of the 11th International Conference on AIDS was "One World, One Hope." Activists and doctors alike took to the stage with exceedingly promising results—a new antiretroviral therapy. On this regimen, individuals who were HIV-positive were displaying an undetectable viral load. Many who had already planned their own funerals now had to decide what they were going to do with their lives.

Twenty-six years had passed since Quinton Booker first came to the cabin in the woods and time had not been kind to the man. With a bushy grey beard and shoulder-length hair, Quinton appears to have passed through hell and back, twice, and in a sense he has.

Larry Kramer once said, "We're living through war, but where they're living, it's peacetime, and we're all in the same country." For roughly the past thirty years, Quinton felt like the entire world was at war and he's been the one living in peacetime. Besides the occasional supply run, he's lived at the cabin since January of '97. That's about nine months before the shit hit the fan.

Before everything ended.

Standing in the kitchen, he pours himself some coffee from a percolator and sips it before setting his mug down. He twists the top off an enormous mason jar full of pills, pours a few into his hand, then downs them. Today's book that he's reading is entitled *Edible Flora and You* and as he turns a page, he hears a scream in the distance. A blood-curdling scream. The kind of scream that keeps you up at night. That kind that tells you something dreadful is out there and you had better be prepared.

THE ONLY SAFE PLACE LEFT IS THE DARK

There was a lot he needed to learn when he first arrived out here, but thanks to the nearby Phoenicia Library on Main Street, Quinton could do just that. Books on preserving food, on first aid, on processing game—all these became the lifelines he needed. Smashing windows was too noisy and they might hear him, so he learned how to pick locks. Whatever he needed to know, there was a book at his local library to provide him answers.

Quinton has everything he needs to survive out here—he's got the cabin, solar panels that sporadically work, and his record player—with headphones, of course. There's the greenhouse, and the root cellar, and living near a modest river granted him a place to take baths and collect water. Above the kitchen table hangs the Act Up poster—the one with the pink triangle that says "Silence = Death." He keeps it up to remember, but also because it makes him laugh. After everything that's happened, silence equals life now. If you can shut the fuck up and keep your head down, you might just make it out of a dog shit situation.

As he sips his coffee, there is a loud knocking on the door and Quinton realizes a dog shit situation is precisely what he's in right now. He drops to the ground and slides over to the window, struggling to get a proper peek at who's outside.

What he discovers is some inbred fuck standing there, thumping on the door. The stranger bangs louder as if someone living in a one-room cabin wouldn't hear a person at their goddamn door after the initial knock. Squatting with his face pressed against the cold wood of the window trim, Quinton tries to play out all the different scenarios. Hoping to find a way out of this that doesn't wholly fuck up his day.

The stranger notices Quinton, and gives him a wave, "Sorry to startle you, friend!" He grins, revealing an absence of teeth. "I was just passing through the forest and saw the smoke from your fire. Thought it'd be nice to see another human being for a change!"

He's clearly not going anywhere, so in the most heterosexual voice he can muster, Quinton speaks up. "Get the fuck out of here."

"That's not very friendly." As he snickers, his lips clap against his hollow gums. "Name's Todd. What's yours?" Searching around the cabin, Quinton realizes he must have left his pistol out by the fire pit. "You out here all alone, friend?" This guy isn't going away. One of them is going to be dead soon—and Quinton's not ready for it to be him just yet.

Attempting his best Stallone impression, Quinton screams, "I'm not your friend! Now leave." Some trees rustle out back. This man isn't alone, and that significantly diminishes Quinton's odds of getting out of this unscathed.

"I don't want any trouble. Was just wondering if maybe you might have something to eat for a hungry traveler." He knocks on the door again and it's clear this is his favorite part of the game they're playing—toying with the prey. "What did ya say your name was?"

After taking a deep breath, Quinton leaps to his feet and bolts towards the back door where his axe is resting. Todd must hear the commotion because he grabs a sawed-off shotgun from his behind and blows a hole in the goddamn front door. Pushing open the backdoor just reveals another toothless fuck with a baseball bat that he plants firmly against Quinton's face.

Did you know you can't eat morels raw—but if you sauté or grill them, they can make a great addition to any stew? Be on the lookout in early spring for black morels, and late spring for white ones.

"Morning, sleepyhead!"

It's been a long time since Quinton has had a hangover, but it definitely feels like he has one now. It's also been a long time since he's woken up next to someone. Glancing around, Quinton realizes he's tied to a chair and there are at least ten of them now. Some hover around with Todd standing in the center, while others are outside at the fire pit. Quinton's mouth tastes like blood, and the rope used to secure his hands and legs is stained a brownish-reddish hue. Something tells him these assholes aren't new to this.

But neither is Quinton.

"If you and your men leave now," Quinton squints, "I'll let you live." Todd and his men laugh. The rope digs deeper into Quinton's wrists the harder he struggles to escape.

Todd turns around to his men and shrugs. "Guess we better leave, boys!" He picks up the baseball bat and slams it into Quinton's gut, knocking the wind out of him. What he doesn't know is Quinton had pneumonia three times in the same year, and this shit feels like nothing compared to that. "We're not going anywhere. Not yet." Todd sees the Act Up poster, the photos of all of Quinton's fallen friends, and the photo of Quinton and Frankie. "Okay, so what the fuck is with all this faggot shit?" He points at the pink triangle and his lips start clapping again. "Are you a faggot?"

Quinton spits some blood on the floor, and it hits Todd's shoe. Todd slides over a chair and sits across from Quinton.

"I'll tell ya what . . . We'll make a deal. You seem like a smart and organized guy. Maybe I would even say anal . . . " His goons laugh as Quinton pictures what they will look like inside out. "A smart and organized guy like yourself would definitely have enough food stored to live this very comfortable life you have out here. And I'm guessing if you're smart enough to have a lot of food . . . You're also smart enough not to keep it in the cabin. Just in case a new friend like myself might show up with his friends."

They haven't discovered the root cellar yet. That's at least one good thing Quinton can hold on to, but it's simply a matter of time. "Why don't you tell me and the boys where you keep the food and then we can be on our way? Let you get back to listening to your little records and whatever else it is that you do here."

"This is your last warning." Quinton peers into Todd's

empty eyes in an attempt to show how serious he is, but knows it won't change anything. Everything that happened with Quinton, with Frankie, with the entire fucking world falling apart—it all led to Quinton and Todd here in this room, in this moment, and it was always going to play out exactly this way.

Todd stands up and crashes the bat against Quinton's face. With his tongue, Quinton feels a tooth come loose and thinks that if this keeps going, he might be able to join their crew of assholes.

"I don't think you understand what's going on here!" Todd begins exploring Quinton's kitchen and notices the picture with Frankie, the one taken on their first date. He rips it off the wall and shows it to the other guys. "Now this is just too precious. I'm gonna hold on to it for now." He puts it in his breast pocket and grins an empty grin at Quinton.

Now it feels like he killed Frankie, and in a way he has because that's the only picture Quinton has with him. Todd shuffles over to the mason jar on the counter. It's the one Quinton keeps his meds in. The one that he's been adding to for years after every supply run. That mason jar is Quinton's fucking life. "It must've taken you a long time to collect all this. And something tells me they ain't aspirin."

He smashes the jar down on the floor, and Quinton watches as his future is shattered and stepped on and pushed into the floorboards. "Oops!" He crushes every capsule and makes sure there's nothing left but powder. With the photo of Frankie, Todd has taken away Quinton's past, and now with the meds, he's taken away his future too. Quinton can't wait to get his hands on him.

Before Quinton can figure out how to do that next, Todd nods to one of his men who slams the bat against Quinton's head again and while everything is going black, Quinton struggles to keep conscious, and has only one thing on his mind . . .

If this is it, what a fucking waste.

CHAPTER TWO
Spin Me Round

"YOU OKAY?"

It's dark out now and the cabin is illuminated bright orange from the fire outside. They're still here, but so is Quinton. Sitting across from him is a nervous young guy. He fidgets and shifts his weight, all while keeping Quinton's pistol aimed at him.

"What are they going to do to me?" Quinton's entire body hurts, especially his face, but all he can think about is the powder on the kitchen floor. And Frankie. That fuck took Frankie.

The kid shakes his head. "I don't know." Quinton worries the gun is going to go off. He's gripping it so tight.

On their first date, Frankie told a story about how he was once almost mugged. He was carrying a wad of cash with him for an apartment deposit when a group of men started following him. They kept looking around, like they were trying to make sure no one else was around, that there weren't any witnesses. He knew how screwed he'd be if he lost that money, so he did the only thing he could—he pissed his fucking pants and started crying like a pathetic baby. The guys ran away, and Frankie got to keep his money. He just had to do an extra load of laundry. When he told Quinton that story, it was the moment Quinton fell in love with Frankie. Most men, especially gay men, never want to show any kind of weakness. But Frankie? He weaponized it. He became Quinton's hero, and now it was Quinton's turn.

He isn't sure what the kid will notice first—the smell, or the growing pool of urine charging towards him. Quinton releases the waterworks.

"I'm so scared." With more tears, the kid stiffens and tries not to make eye contact. "After everything I've been through . . . This is where it ends?"

"Come on, man. Don't cry." He notices the pool and scoots himself back a bit.

Quinton lunges forward onto his knees, which are now covered in piss. "Please! You could let me go! I'll leave out the back and never return. You guys can have the cabin! I don't care anymore, I just want to live!"

Now Quinton can tell he's got the kid exactly where he wants him—he'd do just about anything to get Quinton to stop fucking crying. "Fine! Calm down." After placing the pistol on the ground, the kid gets out a pocketknife and opens it, then cuts Quinton free. The assholes are enjoying themselves by the fire pit as Quinton sneaks over to the window. "I might even come with you." The kid chuckles. "I ran into these guys last week and didn't realize they were this cra—"

His warm blood gushes over Quinton's hands as he shoves the knife into the kid's throat.

"You ran into the wrong group."

Back at the fire pit, the assholes have no idea their boy is gurgling his last few breaths. Looking through his records for the right mood setter, Quinton comes across Dead or Alive's *Youthquake*. He and Frankie would play this album on a loop for hours as they lay in bed, talking about where they were and where they wanted to go in their lives. The future was a mirage and, for a brief time, they bought into it.

When Todd and his gang first came across Quinton's cabin, they probably thought they had struck gold. The solar panels alone meant there was a chance at having some semblance of a normal life. What they probably hadn't noticed was sitting next to the solar panels on the roof were speakers. Big speakers. Their gold is about to be their death as Quinton unplugs the headphones and starts the record.

Pete Burns doesn't get one word out before Todd and his men are all running towards the cabin. Quinton grabs his pistol and a claw hammer off the table as he bolts towards the back door. A large man greets him and tries to enter the cabin, but Quinton swings the peen of his hammer, practically tearing the man's head in half as it rips down.

Another man jumps out in front of Quinton, and is thrown to the ground as Quinton raises his hammer towards the sky, then brings it down and hits him again and again and again, so many times the head of the hammer breaks off. When another man grabs Quinton, he turns around and begins stabbing him with the broken end of the handle.

After that, Quinton runs into the darkness of the forest. The forest, by this point, is fucking screaming. They're coming. The Afflicted. Todd and his men are done.

In the October 10, 1997 edition of the *Washington Post*, there was an article on page one entitled "NEW STRAIN OF RABIES-LIKE VIRUS FOUND IN THE LOS ANGELES AREA." In it, author Dylan Bernbaum noted the "strain is unlike any found before. It seems to take control of the central nervous system, but does not kill the host." The article continued: "It is unclear whether this is actually a parasite or a virus. But it appears to spread through blood and saliva mostly by bite and its effects are almost immediate."

The now-dead Bernbaum wrote, "It is equally devastating to both men and women alike of all races and classes." This was the first mention of the disease that would eventually take out 75% of human life on earth. It never got a name, because there wasn't time to name it before everyone was gone. No cure or treatment was coming.

Just like poor Frankie all those years ago, all they had was skin to hold their bones. With their tissue slowly rotting away, every movement threatened to tear them open. Creating a gash that would never heal. Their hopes, their dreams, their memories, all of those were still there.

They aren't dead yet, but they aren't alive either. The Afflicted are still conscious. They can feel, and they can scream. They can beg for death. But they can't move their own bodies anymore. That job belongs to the virus now.

△

"Please kill me!" one of the Afflicted begs as Quinton picks up his axe and plants it into the poor bastard's skull. As Quinton works his way through Todd's men, and the Afflicted, and Todd's men who have turned into the Afflicted, he's keeping his eyes on the prize—his toothless friend running deeper into the forest, screaming and crying.

Quinton's not done with him yet. Todd has Frankie, and Quinton wants him back. One of the Afflicted jumps out in front of him and screams, "I'm sorry!" Quinton grabs it by the hair, but its scalp rips off as its body falls to the ground. He slams his foot down and its skull shatters almost immediately into a stew. Its last word is, "Yes!"

Todd runs through the dark forest, dodging creatures from all directions. He turns around to see Quinton behind him, covered in blood and piss and filled with rage. Todd raises his shotgun, ready to take Quinton out, but Quinton quickly throws his axe at Todd. It hits him in the shoulder, sticking out like it was always a part of him. Todd squeezes the trigger as he falls to the ground.

The shotgun illuminates the forest for only a moment, and then the pellets nick Quinton in the leg as he screams.

THE ONLY SAFE PLACE LEFT IS THE DARK

He regains his composure quickly, and limps over to Todd, ripping the axe out of his new friend.

"You fucking faggot!"

Quinton pulls some rope out of his waistband and wraps it around Todd's torso, hitting the wound as many times as possible. "Just kill me, you sick fuck!" Todd's voice cracks as he searches and prays for one of his men to come save him.

"I said if you left, I'd let you live. I didn't say I'd kill you if you stayed." Quinton smiles as he ties Todd to a nearby tree.

"Please! This is wrong!" Quinton dips his hand in Todd's breast pocket grabs the picture of him and Frankie.

"We really were precious." Smiling at Todd, Quinton whistles, then limp-runs back into the forest.

Todd's practically hyperventilating now. "Come back, you sick bastard!" His screams are just attracting the Afflicted though, and by the time he realizes this—it's too late. One of them runs up to Todd, begging for forgiveness at what they both know is about to happen. Its teeth tear into Todd's wound, making it larger while both Todd and the Afflicted scream in horror together at what is taking place. As Todd's blood pours into the Afflicted's mouth, they both think about how this is the first time either of them have been held by another in a very long time.

But Quinton only has one thing on his mind . . .

What a fucking asshole.

CHAPTER THREE
Jet Lagged

THE KID'S BODY bloats after two days. Maggots dance on the surface of his flesh while having a full-on house party inside.

It smells like shit in the cabin, but Quinton has more important things to worry about. His left pupil swims in a pool of blood. His thigh is riddled with holes from the shotgun, and he puts a towel in his mouth as he pours alcohol on the wound. For a moment, as the blood washes away, he's able to see the full extent of the damage and it's not pretty, but as more red seeps out of the tiny craters, he's able to push that to the back of his mind.

What.

a.

fucking.

asshole.

Quinton has a sip for himself, then reaches over to the table to grab some pliers. He takes a deep breath and then gouges them into his thigh to rip out all the pellets. One by one, he screams into the towel as he pulls the little fuckers out. Each one causing more pain and more blood. Each one causing more anger.

Next is the needle and thread. The big fucking needle and thread. He holds the large needle over a candle and then plunges it into his skin. Then out again. Then in again.

Once finished, Quinton tries to make it over to his bed,

but falls short and just lies on the ground. Another deep breath and he closes his eyes.

△

It's dark out now. He must have been asleep for hours—or was it days? His leg hasn't stopped bleeding, but it's slowed down now, at least. There is a small pool on the ground surrounding him. It's getting sticky as it dries. Quinton fights through the pain as he drags himself up onto the bed.

Every move is excruciating.

In the distance, Todd continues screaming.

Quinton closes his eyes again.

△

Morning. Todd's still at it—the whiney little diva.

Quinton's been laying awake on this fucking bed for about an hour already. The pain hasn't gone away, and neither has the reality of the situation. His attention briefly goes to the broken glass from the mason jar on the floor. Then at the kid. Then at the ceiling. *Fuck*. It's a lot easier just staying in bed, but he's done enough of that for a while.

Quinton pushes himself along the ground using his good leg. He drags the kid's body by the foot until they are both out of the cabin. Taking a moment to compose himself, Quinton spots the red children's wagon he uses to collect firewood, and drags himself past the multitude of dead bodies—both human and Afflicted alike. He throws all the firewood off the wagon and then lifts himself up into it.

While holding the handle for steering, Quinton uses his good leg to push himself into the forest. The process is very monotonous and painful.

Todd is still tied up to the tree. He is now bloated and decomposing as well. Every time he screams, a large cluster of flies disband, then quickly return. Their main priority right now is his eyeballs, but they spent a good portion of the night on his open wound. He could feel every bite, every flicker of a wing. He felt it all. Quinton passes Todd's corpse in his wagon.

"Kill me! Just fucking kill me!" His mouth can't move, but his voice is hiding in his throat.

Quinton stops rolling for a moment, and remembers Todd's shotgun, the shotgun that has him in this situation right now. Todd stops crying for a moment, and Quinton drops the gun into his cart. Todd cries some more as Quinton rolls himself away.

Years ago, when Quinton first put the red ribbon on the tree, he thought it might be a bit on the nose. It stood out in the middle of the brown and green forest, and today he is glad that he did it. Today, the last thing he needs to be worrying about is finding a single tree in the middle of a sea of trees.

Quinton digs at its base. After getting about half a foot down, he sees a small metal lunch box. There are two bottles of pills inside. He pops open a bottle and downs a pill, then puts the bottles in his pocket.

"Help me!"

"God damnit, Todd. Shut the fuck up already! I get it!" While trying to do the math in his head of how many pills he has and how many days he has left, he smells it. It's been dead a lot longer than Todd and the stink is getting stronger and stronger. Quinton turns around and sees it. Probably a straggler from a few nights back. Quinton scrambles to the cart and grabs the shotgun. He cocks it, but it's stuck.

"I don't want to do this!" The pain in their voices always throws Quinton off. It's something he never wants to experience himself. He finally cocks the shotgun successfully with the Afflicted just about to pounce on him. He squeezes the trigger.

Its head disappears and its body falls lifeless onto the ground. Red mist fills the air before dissipating. Quinton is near hyperventilation now, but looks down at his leg. The stitches have ripped open and blood seeps through his pants.

"Fuck you, Todd!"

Quinton sits in the kitchen with his leg elevated on a spare chair. He drops a handful of 9mm bullets onto the table and begins taking them apart with his knife. The knife he used to kill the kid. He pours the gunpowder out onto a piece of paper, then carefully pours the gunpowder over his wound.

He bites down as hard as he can, then lights a match. The gunpowder ignites and his thigh blisters then blackens.

He takes a swig of whiskey from a blood-stained bottle, then pours some on his thigh. Quinton grabs some clean bandages from a first aid kit and wraps the wound. He makes his way to the bed—not far away thanks to the small footprint of his cabin, but still far enough to make this a painful process. He keeps his bad leg on the chair and drags himself over to the bed, where he plops himself down and passes out.

The front door swings open and Quinton slowly exits his cabin. He has fashioned some branches into a crutch to assist his walking. His leg still hurts like hell, but the time for rest is over. A pack of coyotes gnaw on the bodies scattered about the property. There must be at least twenty rotting corpses if you count the Afflicted. This is the feast the canines have been waiting their entire lives for. Quinton picks up a nearby rock and throws it near the coyotes. They scramble.

One by one Quinton piles the bodies on top of one another in the fire pit. As the flames ignite, Quinton must stand back as the blaze is almost too much. He hates burning bodies. It always reminds him of this party he and Frankie went to one time. Before it all went to shit. There was this hysteric queen screaming and crying, insisting that soon the government was going to start burning all of their bodies. *Our* bodies.

That queen is dead now, and so is everyone else who was at the party.

THE ONLY SAFE PLACE LEFT IS THE DARK

Later, in front of the mirror, Quinton holds the knife up to his hair. One of Todd's men grabbed him by the hair the other night, interrupting his slaughtering, and he can't let that happen again. After he cuts it all off, including his beard, his reflection is a shock. Jet lag from another time and a relic of who he once was, and a reminder of who he is now.

He plops a phonebook down on the table and searches for pharmacies. As he finds the new addresses, Quinton marks them off on a map. There are several pharmacies already crossed off, because this has become a ritual of his over the years. Whenever on a supply run, he hits up one of the pharmacies and gets whatever meds are left. These small towns never had much need for HIV treatments, so he's yet to hit the jackpot. A few bottles here or there have always kept him going. But after the loss he had the other day, Quinton will need a jackpot if he wants to survive. Then he wonders if surviving is even something he wants to do anymore. He's done it for so long and look how quickly all that went to shit. But he has to. He knows that.

With survival on his mind, he gathers up a few of the basics: jars of preserved fruits and vegetables, flashlight, the remaining pills, extra bullets and shotgun shells, and a first aid kit.

The last thing he grabs is the picture of him and Frankie.

The uneven ground on the floor of the forest is a painful reminder that he's not out of the woods yet with his leg. Quinton tries to take it slowly, but is also eager to finish the journey he is just starting so he can get back to the cabin and his routine. The vast upstate New York woods Quinton has taken refuge in eventually end and an interstate highway begins. As he leaves the woods for what might be the last time, he glances back and, after only a moment of second thought, proceeds onto the highway.

CHAPTER FOUR
Postcards

Highway 28 no longer belongs to civilization. The road is covered in high grass and plants have overtaken many of the vehicles that were, at some point, abandoned. Some vehicles are empty, while others have skeletons in them. Some have families of skeletons. Postcards from the past, leaving a haunting reminder of what was lost.

Still walking with a slight limp, Quinton moves with purpose and direction. He never enjoys leaving the forest for a variety of reasons, but one thing he does like about the highway is the clear view of the surrounding area. No trees obstructing what is to come in the near future. He can see down the highway and it seems to go on forever.

As he enters the small abandoned town, he remembers back to when he and Pauline first stopped in on their way to the cabin. The Ching Family Pharmacy was on main street and Pauline had to convince the woman behind the counter to let them use the bathroom. After all these years, he never checked here for meds because he didn't want to disturb it. It was one of his last memories of Pauline and he wanted to leave it sealed. He figured she'd understand, given the circumstances.

After setting his backpack on the ground, Quinton gets out his lock pick set and gently inserts the tension wrench into the keyhole. Once secure, he wiggles the rake pick in and, after a bit of struggle, he hears a click.

A mastaba is a type of Egyptian tomb, and in English it translates to "eternal house." This is old air, it's sour. The door hasn't been opened for almost thirty years, and something has rotted in here a long time ago. Quinton clicks on his flashlight and trudges down the center aisle. He can hear something—it's quiet at first, but it's definitely there.

It's the sound of a woman sobbing.

The light illuminates shelves that are mostly empty besides greeting cards and other worthless items never to be used. Every step Quinton makes is calculated as the crying gets louder and louder. This poor woman is hiding behind the counter, crouched in the fetal position. After three decades, even the virus is worn out and so she just lies there, sobbing as her body slowly rots. Quinton stops and gets out Todd's shotgun. He closes his eyes for a moment and then loudly cocks the weapon, ready for action.

The crying woman hears this and jumps up. She sloppily attempts to climb over the counter, her skin peeling off against the surface.

"Kill me! Please!" One of her ankles snaps with all her weight on it and she falls onto the counter and continues to crawl and destroy herself. No matter how long you live in this world, this is not something you can get used to.

With his knife, Quinton walks over to the poor woman. He pushes her head down against the counter, then slowly pushes the knife into her temple. The struggling stops. The crying stops. She is now at peace. Or at least no longer suffering.

Quinton lets her body fall to the floor, then climbs over the counter and almost slips on the loose skin shed in a pile on the ground. After getting his balance back, he walks over to the drawers filled with medication. He rifles through the many prescriptions that were never filled, occasionally grabbing some antibiotics or painkillers, then he removes a drawer out of the wall and kneels, bringing it to the ground so he can start going through his findings.

There are two bottles of Combivir and that will keep him alive for another two months. He opens them and empties their contents into a fresh mason jar, then puts that in his backpack—leaving the empty bottles on the ground. One benefit of the apocalypse is you can make a mess and never have to clean it up.

Quinton knew he was being followed for about twenty minutes before he decided to do something about it. As he makes his way through the cars, he plays out the different scenarios in his head. Waiting for them to do something, Quinton is confused why they haven't yet. They're just following. The figure doesn't seem to be in a rush, and doesn't even have a gun drawn. They're just following.

Quinton decides it's time to end this. As he turns around and raises his pistol, he shoots at a car window next to this person. He sees a man of average height, black, a beard, and medium length dreadlocks. The man ducks behind a car with his face pressed against the hot metal.

"If you were trying to follow me, you're not very good at it!" Quinton keeps his gun raised, ready for whatever might be coming.

"Jesus! I just want to talk!" The man's not even trying to hide that he sounds afraid, and it throws Quinton off. No one has shown their fear to him in a very long time. Besides the Afflicted, of course.

"Why are you following me?" Quinton scans the landscape to make sure they are alone.

The man stays hidden behind the vehicles. "I had to make sure you weren't with a group." Quinton pushes forward, getting closer to this man as he continues to nervously explain himself. "I saw you at the pharmacy."

Quinton hides behind one of the cars. "I left a lot of stuff. If you need something, go back and get it. The place is clear now."

"I think you have what I was in town for." Quinton peeks over the hood and the man isn't moving closer. He's planted behind a car and doesn't seem to be going anywhere until it's safe.

"Oh yeah? And what's that?" Quinton rests his pistol on the hood as the man's hand raises to show something. He has a pill bottle in his hands.

"Combivir."

Fear suddenly fills Quinton's eyes as they dart around in all directions. He grips Todd's shotgun, ready to use if this is some kind of trap.

"Are you with Todd?" He moves forward another car. "I killed that fucking asshole and I'll kill you too!"

"I don't know any Todd." The man is silent for a moment. "I just want to talk." The man stands up, with his arms above his head. He slowly walks towards Quinton—who, with his pistol drawn, shoots another car window. "You really need to relax! You're wasting bullets. And we don't want to attract them."

"Next one will be in your head!" Quinton knows that sounded cheesy, but he wants this man to go away.

"I just want to talk." The man moves closer with his arms still in the air. "Face to face."

Quinton stands up and keeps his finger on the trigger. He walks over to the man, who now has a smile on his face. "See? That's much better. Less stressful."

Quinton is still very stressed. "I'm a quick draw. Don't fuck with me or I'll kill you in a heartbeat." He sounds like he's in some cowboy movie from the 50s, except even gayer.

"I have no intention of fucking with anyone, sweetheart." He puts his hand out and Quinton keeps his distance. "I'm Billy."

"Okay, get on with it . . . And don't call me sweetheart."

22

THE ONLY SAFE PLACE LEFT IS THE DARK

"I think we are both looking for the same thing . . . and I know where to find it. A lot of it." Billy's got his attention, but Quinton tries to play it cool. Billy continues his sales pitch. "You going to just hit up all the pharmacies in the area, right? What are you going to find? A few months' worth? Then what?" Quinton knows Billy is right and Billy senses this. "I'm talking a whole heap." Billy definitely has Quinton's attention.

"What do you mean?" Quinton hates that Billy has his attention.

"Mayner Pharmaceuticals. The company that produced it, they had a warehouse just outside Bridgeport, Connecticut."

Quinton chuckles. "Connecticut? That's like 300 miles away."

Billy nods. "If we leave now, we could make it in a few days. A week tops. I admit it's a huge trip. But the reward would be substantial. After we get the meds, we can part ways and you never have to see me again." Quinton knows there's a catch. There's always a catch.

"Why are you telling me this? Why not just go on your own?" Billy leans against a car.

"Neither of us are young men. The chance of getting there safely on my own is slim to none. And looking at your leg . . . and eye . . . well, everything really . . . I would dare to say you're in the same boat. But if I had someone with me . . . " There it is.

Quinton starts laughing. "You want me to protect you?"

"Yes! And I'll protect you."

Quinton imagines all the small pharmacies he'll have to go to. All the sobbing women with peeling skin. All the chances to die. "How do we even know someone hasn't cleared the place out already?"

Billy shrugs. "I guess we don't."

"And how do I know you aren't just going to kill me after we get to the meds?"

23

Billy shrugs again. "You don't . . . And neither do I."

Quinton doesn't like this. Billy puts his hand out again. "What's your name?"

Quinton hesitantly grabs Billy's hand and shakes it. "Quinton."

Billy's grin goes away because off in the distance, a group of Afflicted are running towards them. Quinton's shooting must have gotten their attention. There are about ten of them, and they are all screaming.

"Please run, I'm coming!" One of them pleads, "I can't do this again!"

Quinton and Billy begin to walk backwards, their eyes still on the cluster of corpses running towards them at full speed. Billy turns toward Quinton. "I know a place we can get to . . . a farm house up the road."

"How far up the road we talking?"

Billy winces. "This won't be fun."

The two men sprint off the desolate highway and into a cornfield. The leaves of the cornstalks cut at their arms and faces. Sounds of the Afflicted pushing through stalks themselves act as a strong motivator to keep moving. One of the Afflicted's legs break as they run, but that doesn't stop them—they fall to the ground and keep dragging their body along, tearing their skin along the rough terrain.

They can see the farmhouse in the distance and Billy shouts to Quinton as they run, "We're leading them right to it, we're gonna have to keep running or kill all of them!" Quinton turns to see the monsters running toward him.

"Once we get out of this, let's see how many there are!" The sounds are getting closer, just as they are approaching the end of the cornfield.

"Get ready!" Billy shouts to Quinton as they break through the finish line out in the open. Both men turn around and draw their weapons as the Afflicted run toward them.

"Watch out!" one of the Afflicted warns as it runs at Quinton, who raises his shotgun and fires. It falls on the ground as more climb over it. Another one runs at Billy, and he fires two shots into its head. There are more here than they had initially thought, and it's starting to get to be too much.

Quinton is surrounded by three of them now, and he shoots one and turns to the next—CLICK—out of ammo. He jabs the shotgun down the Afflicted's mouth and pushes it to the ground, then repeatedly shoves the barrel in and out of its throat until the top of its head breaks off from the bottom.

As he is doing this, one of them grabs Quinton's hand, its teeth break the skin. "I'M SO SORRY!" Quinton stares at the blood gushing out of his fresh wound.

It's over.

This is what he's been running from for the last thirty years. First the plague, and then getting bitten. For a moment, it feels like time has stopped. Quinton stares at his hand as blood slowly pools out of the little slits from the Afflicted's teeth. All these years, and he assumed it would hurt more.

He pulls out a single shotgun shell from his pocket, places it into the chamber, then plants the muzzle against the bottom of his chin. Quinton closes his eyes.

This is it.

Billy sees what's going on and runs over to him.

"STOP! WE'RE IMMUNE!" Quinton looks up at Billy and sees he is holding his shirt up—revealing a long-healed bite mark on the side of his stomach. Quinton's mouth drops open, then he snaps out of it and shoots the piece of shit lost soul mother fucker that bit his hand right in the face.

The last of the Afflicted runs up to Billy, and he throws it on the ground and empties his revolver into it.

Quinton kneels there in shock, unable to move.

Immune?

CHAPTER FIVE
Evolution

QUINTON WINCES AS the needle goes through his skin. Every stitch makes him gasp. He scans the long-abandoned farmhouse as a distraction from the pain. Across the room, Quinton can see into the kitchen. There's a propane stove you'd take camping and a few jugs of water sitting on the counting. Billy must have been staying here for a while now. Quinton and Billy were in each other's orbit and somehow never ran into each other until today.

Billy stops for a moment. "You okay?" He continues sewing up Quinton's hand, wiping away the blood with a cloth after each stitch so he can see what he's doing.

Quinton is at a loss for words. "I guess . . . Confused." Confused is an understatement. For the last thirty years, he's been terrified of turning into one of those things.

Billy agrees. "Understandable. Trust me, I was too." Quinton realizes how long it's been since someone touched his hand. He doesn't know if he even likes that feeling anymore.

"So?" Quinton is eagerly waiting.

Billy stops sewing and shrugs. "I'm not a doctor. I can't explain it." That answer isn't going to do it for Quinton, so Billy sighs, then gets up and sits on a chair across from him. "Clearly, there is something in . . . our virus that . . . you know . . . That doesn't play well with . . . " He motions outside. "That one."

27

"That's all you got for me?"

Billy laughs. "That's all I got for me too, honey." Quinton stares into the fire and thinks about how much he hates being called honey. Billy continues, "It was quite a shock for me, too. It was about a year in and I was traveling with a group . . . We were swarmed and there was no way out." Billy rubs his hand against the scar on his side, reliving the trauma. "We all got bit that day, some of us more than once . . . and we all walked away from it." Billy puts his head down. "Except for one."

"Where's the group now?"

"You know how things are out there. Some left, some were killed." Billy chuckles. "One lucky bastard died of a heart attack."

"And you were all gay?"

"No, not all of us. I ran a house for people living with HIV, and when everything fell apart, we all just kind of stuck it out together for as long as possible." Billy stares at the crackling fire.

"Did that make it easier?" Quinton asks.

Billy is confused. "Made what easier?"

Quinton points outside. "That."

"Community always makes things easier, doesn't it?"

Quinton shrugs. "I wouldn't know."

They sit in silence for a moment, then Billy leans forward. "And what's your story, mister?" He gets back to sewing up Quinton's hand. "How have you been living in this world for twenty-six years and not know that we're immune?"

Quinton doesn't even know where to begin, but tries. "I moved out to the woods about a year before . . . everything. Besides a few supply runs, that's where I've been ever since."

"You've been alone in the woods all this time?" Billy sits there in shock, staring up at Quinton.

Quinton nods. "Until some inbred fuck nugget and his inbred fuck nugget friends came and destroyed my stash of meds."

"What about your people?"

Quinton shakes his head. "No people. Not anymore." He stares at the fire, remembering. "Not for a long time."

Billy glances up at Quinton—is that respect—or pity? Either way, he's done with the stitches. He lightly pats Quinton's hand and then returns to his chair. "I don't know how you could've been alone for all that time."

Quinton shrugs. "I look at the virus as being part of evolution." He can tell Billy has no idea what he's talking about, so he continues, "Humans were so focused on pointless things like money and love."

Billy laughs in disbelief. "Pointless things like love?"

"Money and love are the causes of pretty much every war." He thinks about his statement then nods. "We all would have eventually killed each other, anyway. So this virus just sped up the process and got those remaining to prioritize the more important things."

Billy is trying to process this as Quinton stands up. "And what are the more important things?"

"Survival." Quinton motions towards the boarded-up windows. "Is it safe for us to sleep here tonight?" Billy smiles. "Okay, I think I'm gonna go to bed then." Quinton walks to the doorway, then stops. "Thanks for stitching me up, doc."

Billy winks. "All in a day's work."

They stare at each other and then Quinton goes upstairs. Billy stays by the fire.

Quinton enters a bedroom, and after making sure its empty, he locks the door—just to be safe.

"You don't have to stay here."

It's dark out, and Quinton grips Frankie's hand as if he might fly away.

"Yeah, I do."

Frankie tries to lift his head, but doesn't have the energy to do so. Something's on his mind and Quinton can always tell when something is on his mind, so he just comes out with it. "I got one of the nurses to call my parents today." Quinton tries to hide how much this hurts—he could have done that. Frankie shrugs. "They hung up."

"I'm sorry. Want me to try again?"

Frankie shifts his weight in bed. "No use. Anyway, I got you." Their six-month anniversary is coming up soon, but they both know he won't live to see it.

Quinton kisses Frankie's small, withered hand. "Yeah. You're stuck with me. Now try to get some sleep."

Frankie isn't ready for sleep yet. "My dad and I . . . we used to be close, you know?" It hurts to swallow, and his throat is so dry he worries it will shatter if he coughs too hard. "He was a delivery driver and would always bring me along on his jobs. Everyone called me Mini-Jorge because we were just always together. Sometimes he'd let me sit on his lap and get behind the wheel. I always thought that was the coolest." Quinton listens as Frankie continues, "I was around twelve when I started to realize how different I was. And he noticed it too. Everyone did . . . We didn't spend too much time together after that."

Quinton wipes a tear away from Frankie's eye, then squeezes his boyfriend's hand. "He loved you. He still does."

Frankie closes his eyes. "I think he hates me."

"He just doesn't understand you."

Frankie nods, and Quinton stares out the window again. They hadn't even been together for a year and neither of them wanted it to end. Even if every moment was hell. It was their hell. Quinton hears a noise. It's a mixture of wheezing and crying.

Quinton squeezes Frankie's hand tighter, but just gets a handful of mush. He looks down and all the skin on Frankie's hand and wrist have ripped off and Quinton is holding it. As Frankie begins screaming, the skin on his cheeks rip and tear and his jaw hangs there with nothing to hold it to his face. He's one of them now.

THE ONLY SAFE PLACE LEFT IS THE DARK

Quinton wakes up from the nightmare, and he's covered in sweat. Looking down at his hand, blood in the shape of a bite mark has soaked through the bandage.

He groans and goes back to bed.

CHAPTER SIX
The Nursery

"WAKE UP." Billy slowly opens his eyes to find a shotgun resting on his chin. He tries not to react and instead forces a smile. "May I help you?"

"I don't know how you got in my room last night, but give it back and we can just go our separate ways." Quinton presses the barrel against Billy's chin with more force.

Billy has no idea what the hell Quinton is talking about. "Give what back?"

"My pills. Give me back my fucking pills."

"I don't know what you're talking about." Billy slowly raises his hands and wraps them around the barrel, while looking up at Quinton. "Check my stuff. I don't have them." He motions towards his bag on the ground.

Quinton struggles to keep the shotgun aimed at his new companion as he digs through his possessions. Nothing. "So you hid them somewhere in the house?" Billy shrugs, his hands still in the air. "They didn't just disappear!"

"Maybe you dropped them last night during the chase?"

Billy and Quinton have split up and are walking around the cornfield with their eyes on the ground searching for those damn pills. Billy walks over to Quinton, holding out his hand, which has a pill in it.

Quinton perks up. "You found them?"

"No, but I have a few left . . . Take it."

There's a catch, there's always a catch. "Why would you do that?"

"Because where we're going, there will be tons of pills and we need to stay healthy to get there." Billy extends his hand even closer to Quinton. "So take it."

Quinton downs the pill. "We better get going. There's a hospital about an hour away that we can hit up." He heads back to the farmhouse to get his things.

Billy chuckles. "You're welcome."

△

Quinton walks in front of Billy, still haunted by the nightmare from the night before.

TAP. TAP. TAP.

The sound startles both of them and Quinton raises his hand. "Stop!"

Billy catches up with Quinton. "What is it?"

TAP. TAP. TAP.

Quinton gets out the shotgun and Billy pulls out his revolver. They drop their backpacks in the middle of the road. Billy approaches a car and taps the barrel of his gun against the passenger side window. Nothing.

"Maybe it was just an animal?"

Quinton brushes some tall grass out of the way so he can see inside another car when the window smashes and a bloated corpse jumps out and knocks Quinton to the ground. Its voice cracks. "HELP ME!" Quinton tries to fight the thing off him, but he isn't having too much luck.

Billy rushes over and pushes his gun right against the thing's head. He pulls the trigger and Quinton's face splatters with blood and brain matter. After the initial moment of shock, Billy offers Quinton a hand, but Quinton gets himself up off the ground. He walks over to his backpack.

"You really have a problem saying thanks, don't you?"

THE ONLY SAFE PLACE LEFT IS THE DARK

Billy walks away as Quinton takes out a rag and wipes his face down.

Quinton calls after him. "Thanks for getting blood on my face!"

△

Darkness.

A door opens and light spills into the small gift shop. Quinton pokes his head in and his eyes dart to all sides to make sure they are alone. "This is a bad idea." Quinton kicks a small stuffed animal on the floor.

"Well, I don't know what to tell you . . . We're almost out of meds." Billy nudges Quinton into the gift shop.

"It just feels needlessly risky." Quinton doesn't like this. "I could just take the meds every other day and I'm sure we'd still be fine."

Billy rests his hands on Quinton's shoulders. "We need to do this."

"Can we please be careful, at least?"

Billy grabs a stuffed animal and throws it at Quinton, then laughs.

Quinton ignores this and opens the cash register. He grabs all the coins out of the tray, then kneels next to the door leading into the hospital. He places his ear against the glass to listen for any life or death on the other side.

Billy comes up behind him and waits patiently, whispering, "Anything?"

"Not yet." Quinton places the coins on the ground and then with both hands slowly unlatches the lock, which makes a loud CLICK. Billy raises his gun and Quinton closes his eyes—nothing. He turns to Billy. "You ready?"

Billy nods.

Quinton opens the door slowly. The light stretches across the floor. He throws a coin through the doorway. It hits a wall and ricochets, then rolls along the laminate before finally falling still. The sound echoes through the empty hospital. Then silence. Still nothing. Both men nod to each other and Quinton pockets the change. They turn their flashlights on and enter the hospital.

Their flashlights give only brief glimpses of what must have happened here all those years ago. Skeletons on the floor, dark black blood stains spattered across the walls. Billy puts a bandana over his face to combat the musty smell. After investigating further, the main floor seems like it's all clear. Quinton walks up to Billy and whispers, "There was a gas station across the street, right?" Billy nods. "Meet there . . . If anything goes wrong."

"Nothing is gonna go wrong, honey." Billy pats Quinton on the back.

"Don't call me honey."

They study a directory showing what departments are on what floors. Billy points at PHARMACY—first floor. They walk as if they are on a minefield—each footstep could be their last.

The door to the pharmacy has been practically ripped off and hangs by a single hinge. Not a good sign. They stop in the doorway and move their flashlights around to inspect. Quinton removes another coin from his pocket and throws it into the darkness. It smacks against the wall, then falls on the ground, rolling in place before falling still.

Looks like they're clear. Billy turns to Quinton. "Keep watch. I'll be quick."

"You better."

As Billy enters the pharmacy, Quinton stands at the door, nervously moving his flashlight around to make sure they're still alone. Billy jumps over the counter, and the sound of his feet hitting the floor scares the shit out of Quinton. He pokes his head into the pharmacy. "Hey! Stop it!" Billy smirks at him, and Quinton goes back to guard duty, using this as a reminder of why he's been on his own all these years.

Billy appears in the doorway and shakes his head. "Nothing." Quinton isn't happy, but Billy seems relaxed.

"We just gotta go up to the ICU. They'll have medicine there."

"No! We can just stop at another pharmacy on the way." This isn't how Quinton does things. There's a reason he's still around.

"We've been here for twenty minutes and seen no evidence of life." As Billy talks, Quinton remembers that Billy's still here too. "A hospital will have more pills than some pharmacy in the middle of nowhere. We're here, so let's get what we set out to get."

Billy forces the heavy metal door open and slams against the concrete wall. It sounds like a gunshot that echoes throughout the stairwell. Quinton smacks Billy on the head as they walk in, then they stand still for a moment, listening. After a moment of silence, Billy gets to business. "Okay, so the ICU is on the second floor. This is gonna be easy, trust me."

Quinton rolls his eyes and they walk up the stairs slowly. They make it to the next level and look through the window on the door to the ICU. They see nothing. Quinton is still glaring at Billy, who notices and doesn't care. "We should find you some anxiety medication or something while we're here."

Quinton's glare intensifies as Billy slowly opens the door and peers down the long corridor. Quinton pulls a coin out and hands it to Billy, who throws it down the hall. It hits the ground and starts rolling and rolling and rolling until it stops on a pair of feet. A pair of dead feet. The toes wiggle and their owner begins screaming.

"Fuck!" Quinton slams the door and more Afflicted emerge from rooms and the nurses' station. Quinton and Billy look at each other—this ain't so easy. Screams erupt from downstairs now, too. This is just fucking peachy.

Billy grabs Quinton and drags him upstairs to the third floor. The screams are getting closer. Billy busts open a door and sees no one is in there, so he drags Quinton in. Quinton grabs a nurses' cart against the wall and pushes it down the hallway as hard as he can, then joins Billy. The door closes behind them, and on it is a sign that reads NURSERY.

Afflicted run by, and chase the nurses' cart until it slams into the wall. They keep running past it and into the other stairwell at the opposite end of the hallway. The screams soon quiet to nothing. Billy and Quinton stand still, ears alert.

Instead, they hear something else . . . A baby begins crying. Then another. Then another. Then another. Ten babies, all in separate cribs, all crying for their mothers who died three decades prior. All of whom have been living a life or death of constant pain and suffering for all that time. Quinton can't believe what he's hearing as Billy starts crying and puts his hand on his mouth.

This is fucked up.

Quinton grabs Billy and shakes him out of it. "We need to get out of here now."

Billy pushes Quinton and looks at him like he's a madman. "We can't just leave them!"

Quinton is not doing this. No. Never. Not gonna happen.

"Fine, I'll meet you at the gas station, then." He removes a knife from his belt. Billy begins crying even harder and Quinton knows he can't let Billy do this alone.

"Damnit." Quinton and Billy walk up to the first crib. It's barely human—the eyes had melted away years ago, the skin is like leather. Its little boney arms flail around, unable to do anything. The baby's mouth opens and closes, trying to bite at the air as its jaw bones clap together.

Billy closes his eyes and shoves the knife into the baby's skull. The crying stops. One down . . . Nine to go. Quinton and Billy separate and each take their own row of living nightmares. Quinton walks up to the next one and does it quickly.

Then the next one.

Then the next one.

THE ONLY SAFE PLACE LEFT IS THE DARK

This is fucked up.

Each time he does it, it's as if he's killing part of himself. If there was anything left to begin with. Once he gets to the last one, Quinton covertly wipes a tear away from his face with his shirtsleeve. He turns around towards Billy, who is crying as he ends these poor creatures' suffering. Quinton stares at his last baby that at one point could have become anything. "I'm so sorry." He stabs it in the skull, then just stares at the now lifeless body.

This is really fucked up.

Billy leans in close and whispers. "When I was running the house, there was a woman who lived there a short time, and she had just given birth to a baby girl. Her baby was positive, too. It's worth a try while we're here, right?"

In the medicine room attached to the nurses' station, Quinton searches through the cabinets. He finds two bottles of Combivir.

That's a month for each of them.

CHAPTER SEVEN
Dried Up

"**M**Y FATHER OWNED** a gas station." Billy stands behind the counter, running his fingers along the cash register. The gas station has been ransacked and then some over the years, not much remains but old food wrappers and air fresheners. "I worked there every summer as a kid, and I hated it so much."

Quinton sits on a lawn chair, making sure he still has a view of the hospital. "Did you and your dad get along?"

"No, I wouldn't go that far. We stopped talking when I came out." Billy organizes the male enhancement pills behind the counter. "I had always planned to be angry at him for a few more years, and then we'd fix things . . . But he died before that happened." Wherever Billy is, he snaps out of it. "I used the money from the gas station to buy the house and get it set up." Billy snickers. "That would've pissed him off."

"Family is complicated." After a moment, Quinton corrects himself. "*Was* complicated."

"When you're young, black, and gay in the 80s . . . Most things were complicated."

Maybe Quinton doesn't know as much as he thought. He stares out the window again at the looming hospital, then back at Billy. "I think you really risked our lives today in the nursery." He closes his eyes. "Those things . . . "

"Those babies?"

"Those *things* . . . We should have just left them. We risked our lives for something that wasn't even human. You can't survive if you do shit like that."

Billy sits next to Quinton. "You can't really believe that?"

Quinton shrugs. "We're alive . . . They aren't. It's not like anyone ever looked out for us in the old world." He puts his head down and stares at his feet.

Billy stands up again and walks over to the window.

"That's some bullshit and you know it." He stares at the gas pumps out front. "I used to hate the smell of gasoline when I was a kid." He turns towards Quinton. "Now that it's all dried up, I kinda miss it, you know?" He goes back to the window. "I think I'm gonna try to get some sleep. You?"

"I'm gonna stay up a bit longer." He eats a tomato. "Make sure no stragglers find us."

Billy walks behind the counter and into the back room. Quinton looks out the window at the hospital again.

△

"How long has he been out for?" Nurse Hastings whispers to Quinton, who is fighting to stay awake himself.

He snaps out of it. "I don't know."

She rubs his shoulder and feels the tension. "Want me to bring you back to your room?"

Quinton onto Frankie even tighter. "I'm okay. I think I'll just stay here."

She sits down on one of the empty chairs and leans in towards Quinton. "I could probably get the janitors to bring your bed in so you don't have to sleep on a chair every night."

Quinton shrugs. "They won't even come in to stop the toilet from overflowing. What makes you think they'd bring a bed in?"

This breaks her heart. He can see it in her eyes and it

breaks his too. "I'm sorry. That's not right." Quinton shrugs. "You boys are too young to witness all this ugliness."

Quinton tightens his grip on Frankie's hand. "We're used to it."

"Have you two been together long?"

"No. Well . . . Six months. Is that a long time?"

It didn't used to be, but now it probably would be considered a long time. "You two make a really cute couple."

Quinton knows she's just being nice, but at one point, not too long ago, they were really cute together. Everyone was jealous of them. But everyone is gone now and they are probably soon to follow.

Nurse Hastings writes something on a clipboard before returning it to hang by the door. "Well, let me know if you two need anything."

△

"We should get going." Billy shakes Quinton awake. Quinton catches his breath, then begins getting ready. "You didn't get any sleep last night, did you?"

"Not enough."

△

As the two men walk along the deserted highway, Quinton's eyes stay on his feet. "You okay?" Billy asks.

"Let's not take any stupid risks today, okay?"

Billy rolls his eyes. "You've been cooped up in that cabin for too long. If we play everything safe, nothing ever gets done in his world."

Quinton eyes Billy. "Have you been on the go since all this started?"

Billy thinks for a moment, then nods. "Pretty much, yeah."

Quinton can't imagine this kind of life—always running, always hiding. "Where were you when it all happened?"

"Greenwich. At the house." Quinton's eyes widen as Billy continues. "It was a total mess! We were lucky we got a van for group trips or we would have never gotten out of the city alive." As they walk, Billy asks Quinton, "How about you? The cabin?"

Quinton laughs. "Yeah. I didn't realize anything had happened for almost six months."

"Jesus."

CHAPTER EIGHT

Goodbye.

STANDING IN THE center of Rhinebeck Village's main street, it's clear something happened here a long time ago. Something bad. Buildings are burnt to the ground, others are boarded up. Some have been looted and some look untouched. Military roadblocks await either end of this long street. Skeletal remains are scattered along the sidewalks. Dark brown blood stains from a different time still haunt the area. Billy waits for Quinton to have a plan.

"Coin toss?"

Shaking his head, Billy says, "I'll take grocery, you take pharmacy."

Quinton puts his coin away. "Deal, just try not to get into any trouble, okay?"

"You're the one who always needs saving."

They take opposite sides of the street. Quinton passes a couple skeletons and accidentally steps on one, cracking a few ribs. He stops and inspects them—they're too small. This was a child. He looks closer and sees a small bullet hole in its skull. This one got off easier than the babies at least. Across the street, Billy studies other bones. They share a glance.

What happened here?

The pharmacy is boarded up—a red X is spray painted on the outside. Quinton thinks for a moment, then knocks on the plywood. Nothing. He pulls a hunting knife out of his backpack and then uses it to jimmy the board off. It falls to the ground and Quinton jumps back to dodge it. After the initial jump, he peeks his head inside and sees nothing to be concerned about—it's just a pharmacy. A really dusty pharmacy.

Quinton has his flashlight on as he walks through the aisles towards the back where the counter is. After being in so many small-town pharmacies over the last three decades, they all seem to be exactly alike. But this one feels different somehow. Sadder.

"Hello?" He moves the flashlight around until it lands on a pair of feet floating in the air. Quinton jumps back, then catches his breath and moves the light up to find the feet belong to a skeleton hanging from the ceiling, a noose tied around its neck. A piece of paper dangles out of the skeleton's pocket.

He gets out his hunting knife, climbs up onto the counter, then cuts the rope holding this long-dead man up. The bones smash against the tile floor, raising dust upon impact. Quinton freezes as he waits to see if anything else has risen, but he's still alone. He climbs down and holds up the paper out of the pocket. It's from a prescription pad, and he unfolds it to find only one word:

Goodbye.

Quinton folds the paper back up and puts it in his pocket. He climbs behind the counter, then gets on his knees to go through the medications. After finding some antibiotics, he puts them in his bag.

Three muffled gunshots go off down the street.

"Fuck."

Quinton has the shotgun in his hands as he rushes down the street toward the grocery store. He's not the only one who's heard the ruckus, though. The Afflicted are pounding on the boarded-up doors and windows, trying to break free to see what all the fuss is about. Screams fill the street. One of them smashes through a glass window and jumps towards Quinton. He grabs it by the hair and starts pummeling its head into the concrete sidewalk. "Thank you! Thank you! Kill m—"

He throws the lifeless body down and continues running. Quinton hides behind a burnt car and pokes his head up to see what he's dealing with. A pack of fucking wolves have now swarmed the grocery store. Billy stands in the doorway emptying his revolver at them. One wolf lies on the ground in a pool of its own blood. Three more circle Billy, slowly moving in.

Quinton stands up from behind the car and aims his shotgun at the wolves, but Billy's legs would be in the crossfire. He starts gesturing for Billy to move, but Billy's eyes are glued on the vicious wild animals before him.

Down the street a growing number of Afflicted head towards them. Quinton shouts, "Move!"

A wolf pounces towards Billy and knocks him to the ground. He begins hitting the wolf in the head with the handle of his revolver until it falls to the ground. Now with Billy out of the way, Quinton rushes the remaining pack and shoots one with his shotgun. Its body flies against the wall as the remaining wolf tackles Quinton to the ground, biting at him anywhere it can.

The Afflicted are now at the entrance and are rushing toward both men and wolf alike. Billy tries reloading his gun, but revolvers are a bitch. It's not a quick process. Quinton bear hugs the wolf as tight as he can. Two of the Afflicted start biting at the wolf as it howls and screeches.

Billy finishes loading his gun and shoots one of the Afflicted in the head. He catches his breath, then jumps to his feet, runs over, and blasts the remaining Afflicted huddling around Quinton. All is silent for a moment. Quinton throws the dead wolf off of him.

"What the fuck?" Quinton slowly stands, but he's shaky.

Billy sees more of them down the street. "We gotta get out of here. There's too many." More Afflicted are coming from all directions, and Billy holds up Quinton as he tries to regain his composure, something they don't have time for. "Can you walk?"

There's not time to think, Quinton grabs ahold of Billy. "We need to run!"

Billy surveys the area, trying to form a plan. There must be at least forty Afflicted now, all heading toward the grocery store. Quinton grabs Billy and begins running up the street, dodging Afflicted as they go. They run down toward a side street with a cluster of houses.

As Quinton and Billy run, Billy looks down at the ground and notices Quinton is dripping a lot of blood from the bite marks on his arms. They have a decent lead ahead of the growing horde of Afflicted behind them. Billy grabs Quinton and guides him into a backyard of one of the houses.

They jump over a few fences back towards the main street. In a random backyard, Billy sits Quinton down on a small swing set. He checks the door on the porch. It's unlocked. He motions for Quinton to join him.

They enter the kitchen, and Quinton finds a seat at the table. Billy closes the door and locks it. He closes all the blinds so no one and nothing can see them from the outside.

"I'm bleeding." Quinton studies his arms.

"Shut up!" Billy presses his head against the door. Trying to hear if anything is coming, but it sounds like they got away, for now.

"I'm bleeding a lot." Quinton's face smashes against the table.

△

Each breath Frankie takes is like climbing Everest. Quinton knows this, and it scares the shit out of him. He presses his ear Frankie's chest. His heart isn't having any easier of a time. Quinton thinks back to the first night they were together. The night he fell asleep in Frankie's arms, he had his head on Frankie's chest then, too. He listened to that heartbeat all night. It was the first time in his short life that he actually felt connected to someone.

Nurse Hastings rushes in and grabs Quinton while she whispers, "You have to get out of here." Quinton stands up, confused as she leans in, "His parents just showed up. The doctor is talking to them right now, but they'll be here soon, and I don't think you want to be here for that." She starts trying to drag him out of the room with her. "Please trust me on this one. I've seen this play out before."

Quinton jolts awake on a couch. Billy sits next to him, concerned. His wounds are sewn up with thick blue thread now. Quinton looks up at Billy. "You did this?"

Billy nods. "You're lucky Miss Mabel Watkins enjoyed her cross-stitch."

Quinton lays his head back on the pillow. "I thought that was it for me."

"Me too." Billy agrees. "I wouldn't have made it if it wasn't for you."

Quinton struggles to sit. Billy tries to help, but there isn't much he can do. Quinton turns his attention back to his arms again. He must have been bitten at least ten times—by animal and Afflicted alike. "I look like Frankenstein."

Billy clears his throat. "Actually, it's Frankenstein's monster."

Quinton rolls his eyes. "Snob." Billy holds back tears as Quinton tries to assure him. "We're almost there. We'll be fine." He looks deeper into Billy's eyes. "I'll be fine."

Billy tries to wipe away the tears, but they keep coming. "You better."

Quinton examines the room they're in, it's dark except for a few candles. "Smells like vanilla."

"Miss Watkins really liked candles, too."

Quinton chuckles. "We should get going." He stands up—bad idea.

"I think we should wait until dark. Will be easier to get out of here. And you need the rest." Quinton leans his head back on the couch. Billy stays attentive. "Can I ask you a question?"

Quinton closes his eyes. "Okay."

"What was his name?"

Quinton is suddenly no longer lightheaded. "What are you talking about?"

"Your partner."

Quinton hasn't discussed this with anyone in a very long time. "I don't know what you're talking about."

"That stuff you said about love being pointless . . . " Billy sighs. "We both know that didn't come from nothing. Tell me about him."

Quinton doesn't have the energy to fight this conversation. "Frankie." It's been so long since he even said his name out loud. It feels really good. "He was an actor. Or wanted to be, at least . . . Guess that never happened." Billy puts his hand on Quinton's thigh. "It's funny, we were only together for six months . . . " He faces Billy. "But at the time, it felt like we were going to be together for the rest of our lives . . . " Quinton clears his throat. "We almost were; I guess."

Quinton laughs. It's a sad laugh. "Who knows? If he had survived, we might've broken up and never seen each other again."

Billy shrugs.

"Maybe. Maybe not." He thinks for a moment. "Probably would have broken up."

They share a laugh, but that goes away quickly. "He was so fucking pretentious sometimes . . . " Quinton chuckles. "He used to call non-actors civilians. Isn't that just the worst?"

"That's disgusting." Billy chuckles. "Was Frankie why were you out in the middle of nowhere when everything happened?"

"I don't know." Quinton's eyes are on his feet. "Maybe

50

I just didn't want to lose anyone else. I mean, before Frankie and I were in the hospital, we were going to multiple funerals a month."

"Me too."

"Twenty-year-olds shouldn't lose everyone they know."

"After Frankie, after everything . . . why didn't you just end things? Why go to the cabin and keep going?"

Quinton thinks for a moment. "When I die, he dies."

Billy knows exactly what Quinton means, and it breaks his fucking heart. "I didn't tell you the full story about when I was bit." Billy exhales. "My husband, Patrick. He was with our group."

"What happened?"

"When I got diagnosed, I was sure he was going to leave me. Who would blame him back then? But he stayed, took care of me and was always there. When I got better he even went along with the house for other people like me. He was just . . . Wonderful." Billy closes his eyes. He's back to when it happened now. "It's funny, we were so careful about being safe and if we weren't—maybe things would have ended differently."

Quinton's body fills with dread. "He was negative?"

Billy recites his story again. "We all got bit that day, some of us more than once . . . And we all walked away from it."

Quinton finishes it for him. The hardest part. "Except for one."

Billy holds back tears and nods. "Except for one." Quinton reaches for Billy as if he's about to float away. He grabs his hand, as Billy wipes the tears off his face. "After Patrick, I wanted to run off and die, but the group wouldn't let me."

"You're lucky." Quinton wonders what life would've been like if he had gotten to Pauline in time. If he could have saved her.

"I don't know about that, but I'm here."

Quinton tightens his grip. "We're here."

Mable's bedroom smells like lavender and the bed is still neatly made. She must have made it every morning after she and her husband woke up. Even on that last morning. As they lay down, Billy hits his head against the wall and lets out a yelp. They laugh and continue kissing, they roll over and Billy is now on top of Quinton. He leans back and holds Quinton at an arm's length.

"It's been a long time . . ."

Quinton nods. "Thirty years."

Neither man wants this moment to end. Right now, the entire world is just them. Billy takes off his shirt, and Quinton takes off his. Both men are covered in bruises, cuts, and scars—this is a hard life they lead.

It's been hard for a long time.

Quinton runs his hand along the scar on Billy's side, then kisses it. He feels like a fucking teenager all over again. Billy smirks at this as he pulls Quinton in for another kiss.

A picture of Mabel and her husband sits on the nightstand next to the bed. Both staring on at the display taking place in their bed. Abstract reflections of skin against skin reflect on the glass of the picture frame.

CHAPTER NINE
The Chapel

"**L**OOKS LIKE IT'S** dark out."

Quinton shakes Billy awake and they both smile at one another. It's been a very long time since they woke up next to someone.

Billy nods. "We should probably get going then."

In the dark, the Afflicted wander aimlessly. If one were unlucky enough to run into one or make a sound, they would snap out of it and go for their prey. But until that happens, they just walk around, silently crying to themselves and praying for death.

Quinton and Billy sneak their way out of Rhinebeck Village. No offence to its residents, but they don't plan on returning.

As they walk down Highway 103, the sun begins to come up, and it's a beautiful sight. Quinton always tries his best to remember that there could still be beauty in the world—as sporadic as it may be. On the day of Frankie's funeral, Quinton stayed back so Frankie's parents could be alone. They hadn't told anyone else what had happened to their son, and so they were the only ones in attendance at the funeral. Quinton hid behind a tree and for a moment, he was able to take in the beauty of the fall colors before reality set in again.

Frankie was dead and would never not be dead ever again.

As they walk, Quinton and Billy share a jar of preserved broccoli. They eat with their hands, passing it back and forth.

"My cabin is really nice." Quinton hands Billy the jar.

"Show off."

Quinton laughs. "No, I mean . . . after all this is done and we have the meds . . . you could come back there with me." Billy takes a mouthful of broccoli as Quinton as he continues, "I grow food, hunt, listen to records."

Billy laughs. "I haven't played house with anyone in a very long time."

"I never have."

After thinking about it, Billy stops. "I'd really like that."

Quinton starts walking again. "You better accept my offer. It's not like you have a lot of suitors knocking down your door."

"I don't even own a door!"

They see it from about half a mile back—the large brick building stands out of place against the blue sky and green and brown plantation that has taken over the area. The large cast iron fencing gives the factory a sinister look, like something Cruella de Vil might choose to live in as a summer retreat. As they get closer, it's hard for Quinton and Billy not to notice the two armed guards at the gate entrance. Hiding behind a tree, Quinton points towards the building across the street and Billy nods.

Once in, they climb up to the fourth floor and kneel beside a broken window. Quinton doesn't like this. He doesn't like this one bit. "Maybe we should just go back to the cabin."

Billy can't believe what Quinton is saying. "We might as well jump out this window if that's the option we're going with." He thinks out loud. "I guess we could wait until dark . . . try our luck at sneaking in?"

"What if we just go up to them and explain our

situation? We mean no harm, and I'm sure they're not using the meds."

"You don't just walk up to men holding guns and say you're HIV positive."

They both start laughing. "Yeah, I guess that would be a bad idea."

Then: a voice.

"*Stand up.*"

Billy and Quinton turn around to find two guards with two guns standing behind them. "Slowly."

"We're just lost . . . " Billy nods at Quinton's statement all four know is not true.

"Stand up right now." The guards keep their guns aimed at them as Quinton and Billy slowly stand up.

As they walk across the overgrown street, Quinton wonders if he could take out a guard and get his gun before the other could shoot, but knows that's probably not a good idea. After Frankie and before Billy, death was no longer a deterrent for Quinton. He would do things like that with no concern, but now that he had someone again—someone he cares about—he can't take any chances.

What was once a storage freezer has now been turned into a holding cell. Billy and Quinton are brought in, and a guard motions for them to sit down on a bench. "Wait here." He closes the door after him, and it locks.

Quinton sits on the bench. "Shit." Billy paces around the room, and it's making Quinton nervous. "We should probably get our stories straight in case they question us."

"Yeah? And what do you propose?"

Quinton stands up and gently stops Billy's pacing. "First, I think you need to calm down."

Billy sits down and Quinton does too.

"What's the plan?"

"Simple. We were just looking for shelter and safety, but we saw the armed guards and were worried, so we wanted to get a look at the place from above to see what the deal was." Quinton shrugs, seems simple enough.

"That makes sense, yeah." Billy's calmed down a bit now.

Quinton grabs Billy's hand and holds it tight. "We'll be okay, just relax."

There is a knock and Quinton and Billy quickly move to opposite sides of the small room as the door opens. A chubby man walks in and is way too excited to see them as he regains his composure. "Hi there. Sorry for the guards, but they just have the mindset of protecting more than welcoming." He chuckles to himself. "I hope they didn't scare you too badly?"

"We're good."

"Great! I'm Winston." He puts his hand out and shakes both of their hands. "Nice to meet both of you! I'm the new member coordinator here at the Chapel. Basically, I'm just here to be your friend and guide as you get settled."

"The Chapel?"

"Oh, you don't know? I figured you had heard about us." How the fuck would they have heard about this? "Well, welcome. We call this place The Chapel, but think of it more as a community. We all stand behind Pastor Josie, who's a miracle worker. You'll love her!"

Billy is slightly disgusted, but tries to hide it. "So it's like a church?"

Winston lets out a big belly laugh. "We don't like to think of it that way, no!" It's hard not to like him, even given the situation. "Pastor Josie holds services once a week—they are, of course, optional!"

Quinton forces a smile, trying to come across as easygoing and agreeable. "Sounds really great!"

Winston smiles back. "Potentials like you typically stay for a week or two and then you can decide whether you want to be baptized and join us or if you'd prefer to go on your way."

Quinton nods. "That sounds fair."

As Billy rolls his eyes, Winston puts his arms around his two new friends. "How about I show you to your rooms, and then you can go grab some food?"

THE ONLY SAFE PLACE LEFT IS THE DARK

Winston opens the door to the holding cell and begins walking down the hallway. Quinton and Billy remain in the holding cell for a moment.

"I don't like religion," Billy whispers.

Quinton joins in. "And you think I do? Just keep calm."

Billy isn't budging. "I promised myself a long time ago I'm not gonna hide who I am to anyone!"

"Well, maybe when the religious people have guns, you can make an exception?"

Billy sighs and they follow Winston.

The three men pass the kitchen, which is bustling with activity as a team of ten people cook a sizeable amount of food using portable camping propane ovens. "Our kitchen is making dinner right now, and it smells great, doesn't it?" Quinton is surprised to agree.

The men walk by a classroom with about five children of varying ages. A teacher stands at the front going over a basic math problem. "We have classes for the little ones, and adults are welcome as well if there's something new you'd like to learn."

As they walk through the hall, it's hard not to notice how all the people they pass look happy, and—even more shocking—*healthy*. They get to a small room with a bunk bed in it. "And here's your room, Billy! Sorry, I know it's nothing fancy, but feel free to decorate it however you want."

But to Quinton's chagrin, Billy makes no effort to not hide his sexuality, if anything he leans into it more. "It's more than enough for lil' ol' me!"

Winston uncomfortably stares at Quinton as Quinton angrily glares at Billy. "Okay! Well, we'll let you get settled in and Quinton, I'll show you to your room now."

As Winston walks out, Quinton turns to Billy. "Lil' Ol' me?" Quinton leaves the room and joins Winston in the hallway.

"He's an interesting guy, huh?"

Quinton tries on his best heterosexual voice. "Don't

know him too well . . . " They continue down the hall until they reach another empty room. It's just like Billy's.

Winston shrugs. "Again, it's not much, I know. But it's yours for as long as you'd like it."

Quinton shakes Winston's hand. "Thank you very much. We . . . I appreciate it."

"Glad to hear it! And hopefully I'll see you two in the cafeteria later." Winston turns and leaves the room. Quinton closes the door for a moment, then opens it again and walks back into the hallway, heading straight to Billy's room.

Billy is checking the bed's firmness as Quinton closes the door.

"Why do I feel like we've just entered Jonestown?" Billy sits up.

"We only need to stay long enough to get what we need. They seem friendly enough, though, right?" Quinton definitely wasn't expecting this, but he feels hopeful for the first time in a long time.

Billy shrugs. "We could be hitting up pharmacies right now and heading back to the cabin."

Quinton laughs. "I'm sure it'll be fine. This was your idea, remember?"

"Yeah, but I wasn't counting on religious folk."

Quinton puts his hand on Billy's shoulder.

CHAPTER TEN
Pastor Josie

THE CHAPEL'S CAFETERIA is straight out of a high school. People line up holding trays, being served food through a window. Quinton and Billy stand next to each other in line, and they scan the room. It's an enormous group full of diverse faces.

They see Winston from across the room and he's waving at them, motioning towards two seats he's saved next to him. They wave back. Once the food is placed on their trays, they walk toward Winston and notice everyone smiles at them as they pass.

"Glad you showed up!" Winston motions towards the two seats that he's been saving for his new friends. They sit and begin eating.

Billy talks through a mouth full of food. "We were pretty hungry."

Winston struggles to contain his excitement. "I was talking to Pastor Josie earlier and we are so happy to have so many new friends coming lately."

Quinton nods. "Well, it's pretty rough out there. How long have you all been here for?"

Winston thinks for a moment. "I believe I've been here for three years next month. But The Chapel has been around since Pastor Josie discovered it eight years ago now."

Billy is surprised, and maybe even a little impressed. "Wow. That's a long time for a community to survive."

"We're doing more than surviving, we're thriving! Getting stronger every day."

Quinton glances around the room and notices a skinny woman with long black hair wearing an all white pant suit and long white gloves. She and Winston share a wave. Winston whisper-yells to Quinton and Billy. "That's Pastor Josie!"

Quinton takes a bite. "You know, we would really love to have a few words with Pastor Josie. I gotta admit, I'm so impressed with this place and really want to hear from the person behind it all."

"Pastor Josie loves talking to potentials! I'll see what I can do."

Quinton inhales a bite of the roasted potatoes. "I'd really appreciate it."

Billy grabs Quinton's hand under the table. "We both would."

△

It's nighttime now, and Billy sits on his bunk bed while Quinton paces the room. He opens the door a crack and peeks outside—no one there. Quinton turns back to Billy. "I think we should look around a bit for the pills. If we can get out of here sooner rather than later, I think that would be for the best."

"I agree. This place gives me the creeps."

"Should we split up?"

"No. We're a team, we stick together."

Quinton smiles.

They slowly walk through the empty hallway. Quinton peeks around the corner. A gaggle of guards stand in front of a large door labeled "Loading Dock". The guards talk to one another and are having a good time. Billy is confused. "For such a happy-go-lucky place . . . There sure are an awful lot of armed guards."

Quinton nods. "That's where the pills probably are, and I don't see us getting in there without permission, do you?"

THE ONLY SAFE PLACE LEFT IS THE DARK

"We're fucked, aren't we?"

"Not yet. Guess we'll have to see what this Pastor Josie is all about." Quinton tries to reassure Billy, but he isn't sure himself.

The two men hear footsteps echoing through the halls and take that as their sign that it's bedtime. They each go to their separate rooms.

△

It's the next morning and Quinton lies in bed staring at his bottle of Combivir. For almost three decades, his life has depended on these little pills, it revolved around them. He can remember the first one he took in the winter of '96. Having been through this all before, he was skeptical—pill after pill, combination after combination. But this one somehow worked. It saved his life, or at least kept him alive.

As he ties his shoes, there is a knock at the door, and then it opens. Billy enters. "There's gotta be over 100 people here." As he looks at Billy, he wishes they could have woken up together again. It was nice. Billy continues, "This is probably the biggest group I've seen for at least a couple of years."

Quinton finishes tying his shoes. "Were you in other groups besides the one you started with?"

"A few." His smile goes away. "They rarely lasted very long."

Quinton stands up. "I was gonna walk around a bit and see more of this place in daylight. Wanna join me?"

"Sure."

Quinton kisses him, which takes Billy aback.

"What's that for?"

"Nothing, just felt like doing that . . . It's been a long time since I've felt like doing that." Quinton nods. "It's a good feeling."

Outside, there is a large garden behind the building. It's filled with a variety of plants and there are multiple people working in the field. Harvesting the crop. Quinton

61

shakes his head in disbelief. "Can't deny this place is impressive."

"Yeah, and the people in the room next to mine are a gay couple."

"Really?"

"Guess I don't even get to be outraged about this place being homophobic now." Billy puts out his hand and Quinton grabs onto it.

"I never thought I'd see this many survivors in one place again."

A loud bell rings both inside and outside the building. Everyone stops what they are doing and heads inside. Quinton stops a passing gardener. "Where is everyone going?"

"Time for Pastor Josie's service."

△

Billy and Quinton follow the herd of people walking down the hallway toward the loading dock. It's open now and everyone is going in. They look at each other—be alert.

The loading dock has been turned into a makeshift church. All the pallets of medication have been pushed against the walls to make room for nearly a hundred folding chairs. The chairs all face in one direction—towards a crudely constructed cross with a small podium in front of it. Billy and Quinton sit near the back and they politely smile at the parishioners next to them. Winston is in the front row. He notices his new friends and waves.

Pastor Josie walks into the room and behind the podium, beaming with joy. She wears a loose-fitting white cloak. Her mere presence makes everyone forget about the outside world—except for Billy and Quinton, who are focused solely on the boxes and boxes of pills against the wall.

"Greetings, everyone! Welcome to the chapel. As most of you know, I'm Pastor Josie." She steps out from behind the podium and paces, keeping her eyes on the crowd. "The light of God is watching over all of us today. I know that to be true. One of our search teams found a flock of wild sheep roaming a field yesterday, so we'll be having quite the feast tonight!" Everyone is thrilled and puts their hands up to the metal ceiling. She continues, "Everyone here is working to purify themselves of the evil lives they once led. I, too, at one point, was living a sinful life." She laughs at her past self. "But now, thanks to accepting the lord's light into my heart. I'm immune to hatred." She faces back at the cross and puts her arms out. "And I'm immune to the devil's plague!"

Quinton and Billy share a glance. Everyone else claps. Josie motions towards some guards and they leave for a moment, then return with one of the Afflicted, who is chained up by the neck. Its arms are missing and the wounds have been crudely stappled shut, so as not to get any blood on the ground. It screams out to the crowd, "Please kill me!" The audience is really riled up now. Quinton and Billy are even more confused and concerned. The Afflicted continues. "Why are you doing this? Just kill me!"

Pastor Josie laughs and sticks her arm out in front of the Afflicted's mouth. It can't control itself, it gnaws on her arm. Blood drips down her arm, and it's clear from other scars this crazy bitch does this once a week. Quinton and Billy look at each other—they know her tricks. She tugs her arm away from the poor soul and nods at the guards to take it away. It pleads through its exhausted voice to end things as it's escorted out of the loading dock.

"Now, there are three new people who want to join our community today and so we will do three baptisms!" Everyone stands up to cheer. "That's the most we've ever done in one day! Let's bring them out!" A guard escorts a young family out in front of the crowd. There's a mom, a dad, and a little girl who can't be older than eight. Pastor Josie hugs them and holds the little girl's hand. Josie's arm drips blood onto the girl. The crowd sits down and watches with eager anticipation. "Years before the devil's plague took over, our sanctuary was a pharmaceutical factory. Mayner Pharmaceuticals was the largest manufacturer of fentanyl in the United States." Quinton and Billy share a glance—what the fuck is going on here? A guard walks behind the podium and brings out a nursing cart. "After countless deaths from overdose, Naloxone was introduced to combat such an untimely death."

Three guards push stretchers out and help the young family get onto them. They are then tied down. The little girl is terrified, and so are Quinton and Billy. "I found that in order to accept the light and continue on a path of righteousness, you must first face the light! Face our lord and gain her acceptance!" Everyone claps, but Billy wants to run up there and try to stop this. Quinton grips his hand tightly.

Pastor Josie approaches the nursing cart and picks up a syringe. She plunges it into a small bottle marked fentanyl, she does this two more times. Picking up the first syringe, she walks over to the nervous father. All the applause is helping him feel like he's doing the right thing for himself and his family. Pastor Josie grazes her hand against his cheek and then injects the fentanyl into his arm. His eyes roll back and he passes out.

Billy, almost in tears, turns to Quinton. "Jesus fucking Christ!"

Quinton whispers, "There's nothing we can do."

Through his eyes, Billy pleads with Quinton. "There has to be something."

Pastor Josie hovers over the mother, whose breathing has turned to panting, which now turns to rasping. Josie maintains eye contact with the cross as she injects her. The mother's breathing calms. Quinton leans in close to Billy. "I'm sorry."

The little girl doesn't understand what's going on as much as they tried to explain it to her. As she looks at her mommy and daddy sleeping next to her, she starts yanking harder at her restraints. She stares at the encouraging crowd who sit there and do nothing. None of this makes any sense to her, and she's grown up in a world that makes sense to no one for a very long time.

The Pastor stands next to the little girl, and softly kisses her forehead. "It's okay, little one," Josie says as she slowly pushes the needle into the girl's arm and injects her with the drug. Almost instantly, the little girl passes out.

Pastor Josie looks up at her guards and nods, then they quickly walk over and inject each member of the family with naloxone. The audience stands up again and claps in unison. Quinton and Billy are standing out of absolute terror and concern for these poor people. After a moment, the father jerks awake and is disoriented as the applause gets louder. Then the little girl wakes up as well and begins struggling to get free from the stretcher. People cheer and holler now—this is more like a basketball game than a baptism.

But the mom doesn't move.

Josie feels her pulse. Nothing. The father and daughter look over at their wife and mother and start screaming. Pastor Josie motions to the guards to get rid of this situation. They wheel all three stretchers out of the room. Pastor Josie thinks for a moment, then turns to the audience with disappointment. "Some people just have too much hate in their hearts. They aren't ready to be accepted into God's light." She shrugs, then puts on a big smile. "But now we have two more members in our family!" Everyone stands up and cheers.

Everyone except Quinton and Billy.

CHAPTER ELEVEN
The Deal

BILLY STORMS INTO the room and starts packing his bag, Quinton slowly follows, exhausted. "Come on, what are you doing?"

Billy lets out a laugh and stops packing for a moment. "What does it look like I'm doing? We're leaving."

Quinton closes the door. "It looks like you're making an emotional decision and not thinking this through."

Billy turns and gets in Quinton's face. "An emotional decision? That psychopath just killed that little girl's mother!"

Quinton tries to hug Billy, but he goes back to packing his bag. "Yeah, it's really fucked up! I'm not saying it isn't!" Quinton grabs Billy. "I don't want to be here, either. I don't. But are you really suggesting we leave now?"

Billy backs away from Quinton. "Yeah, that's exactly what I'm suggesting."

"Then what?"

Billy thinks for a moment and shrugs. He sits on the bed and Quinton walks over and joins him.

"Yeah, exactly. If we leave now without these meds . . . we can never stop moving. It'll just be town to town, pharmacy to pharmacy, and we'll never be able to settle down. Eventually, our luck is going to run out and someone or something will kill us. Is that really the life you want?"

"Is *this* really the life you want?"

Quinton puts his hand on Billy's leg. "No! That's why

I'm saying we just need to keep quiet for a little while longer and get through this. I'm not suggesting we join this place."

Billy shakes his head. "Sometimes in life, you need to ask yourself at what cost? What is the cost of what we're doing here?"

Quinton hates fighting. He always hated doing it with Frankie and he hates it even more with Billy. "I don't know. I just know I can't lose you and I want us to go back to my cabin and live out the rest of our lives. That's all I want. Can you please just do this for me? I'm sorry."

△

At the cafeteria, everyone is happily eating, and no one seems perturbed by the service they witnessed earlier in the morning. Quinton and Billy sit at the end of one of the tables. They are scarfing their food down as fast as possible. Winston walks over and kneels down by the two men. "So that was something, wasn't it?"

Billy doesn't make eye contact, he just continues angrily eating. Quinton tries to play ball with Winston. "That was definitely something, yeah."

"It's too bad about Sandra," Winston shakes his head. "I had a good feeling about her, too."

Quinton squeezes Billy's knee, knowing what Billy wants to do. "Do you think we could get that meeting with Pastor Josie now?"

Winston perks up. "Ah yes! I forgot, but I brought it up to her this morning and she sounded really excited to meet you two!"

Quinton puts on a show. "Great!" Billy just stares at his food.

Winston escorts them through an empty hallway. They pass a room to find the father and daughter crying hysterically over Sandra's corpse. The father made a mistake coming here and doesn't know how he's ever going to look at his daughter again. A guard slowly closes the door. Winston continues down the hall.

THE ONLY SAFE PLACE LEFT IS THE DARK

Winston, Quinton, and Billy enter the office and sit down on chairs facing an enormous desk. The office is sparse, and the focus is clearly meant to be on whoever is lucky enough to sit behind the desk. A door opens on the left side of the office, and Pastor Josie walks in. Her cloak is gone and she is buttoning up a white dress shirt. Through the door, Quinton sees that's her bedroom next to the office. Pastor Josie sits down and begins trying to size these new friends up. "Winston told me there were two potentials who wanted to speak with me and I believe it's our job to make you feel at home, so here we are."

"Was that making the family feel at home this morning?" Pastor Josie looks at Billy, then Winston lets out a nervous laugh.

Winston tries to break the tension. "Pastor Josie, I have been getting to know these two gents, and I think they would be a perfect addition to our community. This is Quinton, and this is Billy."

Pastor Josie puts out her hand and shakes Quinton's. She turns to Billy, who hesitantly does so as well. "So did you two have any questions in particular? Or just wanted to size me up for yourself?"

Quinton clears his throat. "Actually . . . we were hoping to have a word with you . . . alone."

Winston leans forward. "That's a pretty unusual request."

Quinton makes eye contact with Josie, then motions toward his hand where he subtly points at the bite mark that is slowly healing. Josie sees this and her eyes widen. She brushes it off. "That's fine, Winston, we're fine. Right, boys?" She lets out a nervous laugh. "Just wait outside and we'll get to know one another a bit more."

Winston seems a bit hurt by this, but gets up and leaves the office, closing the door after him. They sit in silence for a long time, then Josie breaks it. "I have to say, I'm surprised it's taken this long to come across someone else who has the blessed virus."

Billy sits forward. "Cut the shit, lady! You killed that poor woman and convinced everyone here that you're some kind of miracle worker."

Quinton pats Billy on the back. Josie continues. "I was a junkie, and I came here for the oxy when the place was filled with Afflicted. I was bitten and thought that was the end, but I survived. And I realized I survived for a reason. I could help people here. I *am* helping people here."

"Is that what you're doing?"

"Look, we just came here for the meds," Quinton says. "Enough to survive on. We really don't want to get involved in all of this."

"Well, I wish I could help you."

Quinton's nails dig into the wooden arm of the chair. "We saw there is more than enough for the three of us and then still have leftovers."

She shrugs. "Those pills don't just belong to me, they belong to the community."

Billy sits back in his chair. "Well, how about we go show the community our fucking bite marks, then? We could even bring that poor soul out and let it gnaw on us for a while. Make a whole holy show out of it like you did."

Josie clenches her teeth. Quinton tries to reign Billy in. "Look, we don't want to cause any trouble, okay? If you give us the meds we're asking for, we'll leave and never come back."

"Is that a promise?"

"Yes. I promise. We both do."

She side-eyes Billy, as Quinton faces him too. "Fine."

Pastor Josie sits back in her chair for a moment and thinks over her options. "Okay, I think we can work something out."

Quinton is relieved to hear that as he stands up. "How about we go back to our room and pack up and once we get the meds, we can be on our way?"

Josie nods. "I think that would be best."

Josie picks up some paperwork—trying to appear like

she's working. Quinton and Billy begin leaving the office, but Billy stops and walks back over to her. "One more thing . . . " She looks up at him. "I want to watch you destroy all the fentanyl and stop doing that disgusting ceremony, or I'm going to expose you for the fraud that you are." Billy takes a step toward Josie's desk. "No one else will die from that ever aga—"

Before Billy finishes his sentence, he falls to the ground. Blood spits out of his throat as he desperately tries to cover the bullet hole with his hands. All Quinton can hear is ringing, and red, and anger. Josie remains seated at her desk, holding a large magnum revolver. Quinton lunges to the floor. "Billy!" He glares at Josie. "You fucking psycho!"

Winston and two armed guards storm into the office, as confused as Quinton. Josie stands and points at Quinton. "Put him in the holding cell!"

The guards grab Quinton, as Winston watches the life slowly seeps out of Billy, then turns his focus to pastor. "What the heck happened?"

Billy is barely conscious, but awake enough to be scared shitless. He doesn't want to go. Not now. Not like this. The guards drag Quinton kicking and screaming out of the office. "Take me back! I need to be with him!"

Billy lies on the ground in a pool of his own blood. Winston gets on his knees and is trying to check his pulse, but with all that blood, his hand just slides off of Billy's neck. With his breathing erratic, Billy knows this is the end. The breathing finally ceases and now he's just a body on the floor.

The holding cell door opens, and Quinton is thrown inside. It closes behind him and then locks. Quinton can't think straight. He can barely breathe. He kicks and punches at the door, then falls to the ground sobbing.

That was his last chance.

CHAPTER TWELVE
The Blessing

QUINTON RUNS DOWN the hall into Frankie's hospital room. The bed is empty. Frankie's gone. Nurse Hastings is changing the sheets and when she sees Quinton, her heart breaks. "I'm so sorry, honey. He passed last night."

He can't move. "What?"

She walks over and hugs him. Their eyes well with tears. "He's no longer in pain."

"I wasn't there for him. We promised each other we'd be there for the end. Whoever went first."

She hugs him again and clutches him even tighter. "I'm so sorry."

Quinton pulls himself back when the empty bed catches his eye, then runs away as fast as he can.

△

Quinton sits on the ground and is utterly defeated. There's no fight left in him. He just stares at the floor. The door opens and Winston walks in. He sees how dire the situation is for Quinton and kneels down to be at his level. Quinton won't look him in the eyes, but he speaks anyway. "What the hell happened in there? I can't get a straight answer out of Pastor Josie."

Quinton quickly grabs at Winston's arm and pulls him in closer. "That woman is the devil."

73

Winston yanks himself back and falls over. The door quickly opens and one of the guards pokes his head in. "Are you okay in there?" Winston waves him away.

Quinton sits back against the wall. "I couldn't even be there with him before he . . . "

Winston puts his head down. "I'm sorry."

"Why are you even here?"

"I just want to understand." Winston is trying to keep Quinton calm.

"You want to understand?" Quinton pulls his shirt sleeve back to reveal all the bite marks on his arm. He holds it out and displays it to Winston.

"Jesus Christ."

"She's not godly. She just has a virus! She's been lying to everyone and now that little girl is going to grow up without her mother and I'm going to have to go on without . . . " Quinton can't even say the name. Holding back tears, he lunges at Winston and grabs him by the shirt. "All because of that fucking bitch you bow down to!" Winston is terrified. Quinton composes himself and stands up and paces. "We just came here to get medication. The same medication she keeps for herself. He wanted to leave, but I insisted. I believed in this place . . . I believed in you." Quinton paces for a bit, then stops. "What are they gonna do to me?"

Winston shrugs. "I don't know, but she's talking a lot about how much you need to be baptized."

Quinton laughs. "You know what that means."

Winston sadly nods. His entire worldview is crumbling to the ground. "Yeah. Yeah, I do."

There is a knock at the door. The guard pokes his head in again. "Pastor Josie needs you."

Winston shrugs. "I'll be back later if I can."

Quinton laughs at this. Winston walks out of the holding cell and the door slams shut again. The lights turn off. Now in the dark, the only thing he can hear is his angry breathing.

THE ONLY SAFE PLACE LEFT IS THE DARK

Quinton stares at the crack of light from the hallway—having no idea how long he's been in here for. He hears footsteps in the hallway, then the door unlocks and he quickly stands up and readies himself for a fight. The light turns on and it's blinding. As he tries to adjust, the door opens to reveal two guards in the doorway with their guns raised. Quinton puts his arms down, then Winston appears between the two men. "It's baptism time." Quinton stands back in the small holding cell. Winston produces a small pistol and aims it at him. "Give us a minute, okay?" The guards stand back. Winston enters the holding cell and closes the door behind him. He keeps the gun aimed at Quinton. "Don't make this harder than it needs to be. I tried to fight for you. But you are trying to destroy everything we've built here, everything I've built."

Winston stands there, staring at Quinton—waiting for something. Quinton shakes his head. "If you're waiting for my blessing, then you'll be standing here all night." Winston turns and bangs on the door, the guards open it again and raise their guns.

Winston stands behind Quinton with the pistol aimed at his back as they walk slowly down the narrow corridor. The guards stand back a few feet, keeping their eyes on the situation. Quinton faces Winston. "I really thought you were a good person, just caught up in this fucked up situation."

Winston keeps walking. "I could say the same about you."

"Fucking coward."

Winston pushes the small pistol into Quinton's back harder. "I'm a coward? No. I'm a protector."

They pass a wall full of windows. It's dark out, but the moon illuminates their faces. Quinton stops. "Who are you protecting? That little girl? The community? Or yourself and that witch?"

Winston doesn't want to hear it. "Well, this will all be over soon, won't it?"

Quinton nods. "Yeah." He jumps out the second-floor window—shattering the glass and hitting the ground hard. He rolls into the bushes surrounding the building.

Winston and the guards stand there in shock. *What the fuck just happened?* They peek out the window while moving their flashlights around. "I want the perimeter searched and I want him found, okay?" The two guards walk away quickly as Winston stays by the window, moving the flashlight around some more.

Quinton's leg isn't broken, but from the look of how quickly it's swollen up, it's not good either. He drags himself along the dirt, pulling his limp leg behind him and into the bushes next to a window. He can hear the guards in the distance, but doesn't really give a shit right now. His leg fucking hurts. Quinton inches the window open and begins to climb in. His foot gets caught on the windowsill and it feels like someone is ripping it off, but Quinton quickly pulls his foot back as it smacks down onto the hard floor tile. He quietly closes the window just as the guards approach.

Quinton stays pressed to the wall under the window, catching his breath.

From outside the guards flashlights illuminate the dark room, revealing it's where the laundry must get done.

The guards spread out. Quinton drags his bad leg around the laundry room toward a cart full of white sheets. He grabs one of the sheets and rips it into pieces, then ties it around his leg to give it some more stability. It hurts like hell. Quinton opens the door slowly, he sees a guard run past so he closes it again. He breathes deep, then opens it and pokes his head out. From where he is, everything seems clear.

The downstairs is more industrial and less finished than the hallways Quinton was in just a few minutes ago. He limps down the hall, peeking into each door as he goes. He stops and then enters one.

THE ONLY SAFE PLACE LEFT IS THE DARK

The room is small and filled with metal shelves that have backpacks and suitcases on them. Quinton limps around looking at them until he finds what he's looking for . . . his and Billy's possessions. Quinton grabs them off the shelf and brings them to the ground. He first checks to make sure his shotgun and Billy's revolver are still loaded—they are.

He puts Billy's revolver into the waistband of his pants and rests the shotgun on the floor. He opens his backpack and everything is still there. Quinton grabs a bottle of pills, downs one, then returns them to the bag. He looks at Billy's backpack for a second, then sighs. He transfers food, first aid, and pills into his backpack, then comes across a picture. The picture is of Billy and his husband—young and full of hope. Just like the picture of him and Frankie. Quinton closes his eyes for a moment. This isn't the time to cry—he needs to be strong. Folding up Billy's backpack, he puts it into his and then leaves the room.

Quinton enters a stairwell and slowly limps up the stairs. With his shotgun raised, he's ready to obliterate anyone who gets in his way.

Entering the hallway, he doesn't see anyone but can hear the chaos outside. Guards yelling and running around, searching for him. Quinton peeks around a corner at the loading dock door. Multiple guards stand around talking to one another. He turns back into the kitchen.

He finds two spray cans of cooking oil, and carries them over to one of the stove tops. Sitting in the room's corner is a pallet of liquid propane canisters for the camping stoves. He grabs a bottle, opens it, then pours the propane all over the kitchen. Quinton pulls out Billy's backpack and throws a few more canisters of propane in. He turns on two of the burners—one at a low heat, one at a higher heat level, then places a can of cooking oil on each of the burners. He runs out of the kitchen.

Quinton ducks back into the holding cell and waits for what comes next.

The flame from the first burner is heating up the bottom of the spray can, from inside he can hear the oil is sizzling and running out of space. An enormous flame erupts and sends burning hot oil and shards of metal flying into the air. The liquid propane quickly catches on fire as it spreads throughout the kitchen. The smoke dances up to the ceiling and then the smoke detectors scream in distress.

The guards rush towards the kitchen to inspect what is going on. Quinton jumps out of the holding cell and runs down the hallway towards the loading dock just as he can hear the second explosion.

The guards are knocked on the ground as hot oil cooks their skin, trying to put the fire out only pushes the shards of metal deeper. No matter what they do, it means pain.

Quinton slams the door to the loading dock shut and locks it from the inside. He walks over to the pallets of medication and gets out his knife. He cuts the plastic around the pallet and begins loading bottles and bottles of pills into his backpack. Then he produces the propane out of Billy's backpack and loads up even more pill bottles.

This will truly last him a lifetime.

Once he has enough, he sets his bags aside and pours liquid propane over the pallets. He lights a match from his bag and throws it on the pills. No more oxy. And no more Combivir for Josie.

"Please kill me!"

Quinton notices a curtained-off area next to the cross and podium. He walks over and opens it. The Afflicted is in a small cage and once it sees Quinton, it goes crazy. *"What did I ever do to you?"*

The guards bang on the hard iron door, then the lock is undone and it swings open knocking the guards back. Quinton stands behind the Afflicted as it runs towards one of the guards and sinks its teeth into his neck, tearing it open as it pushes to go deeper and deeper. Another guard raises his gun and ends the Afflicted's suffering, but having turned, the new Afflicted lunges at its former friend.

Quinton runs past the chaos and down the hallway. When he reaches the outside of Josie's office, he sees the window on the door is still broken. He reaches his hand through and unlocks the door.

Quinton enters and closes the door. On the ground is a faded stain that someone has been cleaning, but it's not going away too easily. He kneels and runs his hand along the wood grain. Closing his eyes, it's requiring all of his remaining strength not to cry.

Quinton enters the connecting bedroom and closes the door quietly. He tears the curtains open and the moon beams onto the bed that Josie is sound asleep on. He puts the shotgun down on the ground along with his backpack. Pastor Josie has a sleeping mask on. She lies on her pillow, facing the ceiling. A syringe still in her arm and a small glass bottle rests in her unconscious hand—it's oxy.

With knife in hand, Quinton gets on top of her. She wakes and rips the mask off and sees Quinton staring down at her. She's high, but she's aware enough to know she's fucked. Her eyes widen. She doesn't know what to do. Quinton grins. "I wanted you to see who it was that killed you."

Pastor Josie screams, "Guar—"

Quinton starts stabbing her in the throat. He stabs her in the face; he stabs her in the eyes. He drops the knife on the ground next to the bed—it's bent. Quinton gets off the bed and spots the moon through the window and it's beautiful. He wishes Billy was here to see it with him. He wishes Frankie was here. He wishes anyone was here. But it's just him now.

Quinton returns to her office, still covered in Josie's blood. Standing in the opposite corner is Winston, pistol shaking in his hand. When Quinton walks into the light and Winston sees all the red, his mouth drops open. "What have you done?"

"Did you really think I was just going to leave?" Quinton aims Billy's revolver at him.

"You shoot me and everyone's gonna hear it."

Quinton shoots Winston's hand, and the gun clunks onto the ground before Winston can even start screaming. Quinton kicks the gun away and Winston cries as he crawls towards the door. Quinton crushes Winston's bad hand with his boot. "Where is he?"

Winston can barely breathe, he's crying so hard. "Where is who?"

Quinton pushes the gun against Winston's head. "Where is Billy's body?"

"If I tell you, you're just gonna kill me."

Quinton pulls back the hammer. "If you don't tell me, I'm gonna kill you."

Winston closes his eyes for a second. "Down the hall and to the righ—" Quinton didn't need to hear the end of that. He leaves the room, screams still coming from the distance.

Quinton forces the door to the walk-in refrigerator open as he enters. Billy's on the ground. Lifeless. Dead. Next to him is the little girl's mother. Quinton kneels and caresses Billy's face. He kisses his forehead and closes his eyes. After a moment, Quinton slowly picks up Billy's body, then leaves.

Quinton walks down the hallway with Billy in his arms. Multiple guards pass with fire extinguishers and guns, but are too distracted by the chaos he has caused. Screams of the Afflicted are heard in the distance. The loading dock is on fire and is spreading quickly. Quinton and Billy leave this damned place and don't look back.

CHAPTER THIRTEEN
The Cabin

QUINTON BURIED BILLY'S body at the gas station. Their gas station. As he sits there staring at the pile of rocks he placed as a marker, Quinton wonders if Billy would have liked that or not. There's so much he doesn't know about Billy, and so much Billy didn't know about him. That's never going to change now.

Nurse Hastings' black pickup truck drives through the rough terrain and stops suddenly. Quinton gets out on the passenger side and studies the cabin. A few years have passed since Frankie's death, and he reminds himself of this fact constantly. He faces the good nurse. "So, this was your uncle's?"

"Great Uncle." She gets out of the driver's side, wearing a beat-up army jacket.

The cabin is rough. No one's lived here for twenty years. "It's nice, I guess." Quinton grabs his backpack from the trunk and hoists it on his back.

"It'll do for now, but I want you to know I'm only letting you stay here for a year at the most." She wonders if it will even hold up through the winter. "Not because I have any use for it, but because you can't just come here and die."

Quinton rolls his eyes. "Okay."

She grabs Quinton, forcing him to look at her. "Do you

realize how lucky you are? Do you realize how many young men, just like you, I had to watch fade away into nothing?"

Quinton averts eye contact. "You mean young men like Frankie?"

Hastings puts her head down. She lets go of him. "Yeah, young men like Frankie."

Quinton walks over to the cabin and peers through the window—it's fucking filthy inside. "You don't mind if I make some changes? Fix it up a bit, maybe?"

"I don't care. But can you look at me, please?" He turns around and they share a sad smile at one another. "You're not the only person I know who's literally lost everything in this plague, okay?" Quinton nods, but before he can speak—Hastings cuts him off. "*But* . . . you're different. I care about you . . . a lot." She closes her eyes for a moment. "Just promise me one thing."

Quinton is cautious. "What?"

She grabs his hands, holding them tight. "Don't do anything . . . drastic, okay? Things might feel pretty hopeless for a while—maybe for a long while. But you really have an opportunity to start over, and until you can figure out how to live for yourself—can you just live *for him* in the meantime?"

Quinton squeezes Nurse Hastings' hands, then backs away. "I'm not gonna kill myself in your uncle's cabin. I wouldn't do that to you."

She kisses Quinton on the cheek while holding back tears. "I love ya, my darling."

"I love you too. Really."

She walks to her car as Quinton watches her leave. She turns around as she's getting in. "There's a town about an hour's walk that way. There's a pay phone if you want me to come pick you up . . . Just call me. And I'll be around with your meds next month, okay? Stay safe, Quinton."

"You too, Pauline."

She gives him one last kiss on the cheek then rushes over and gets in her pickup. It drives away and leaves Quinton all alone. Exactly what he wanted.

THE ONLY SAFE PLACE LEFT IS THE DARK

△

Quinton makes his way through the forest. He passes Todd—who's really falling apart now. Bugs have burrowed all over his body and he is screaming at every movement. The shoulder where Quinton got him with the axe has been eaten all the way through, and hangs off his body as more of an accessory that a structural component now. Quinton doesn't even look at him. He walks up to his cabin, and is surprised to find it doesn't appear as if anyone has found it since he left. He goes inside.

Quinton sets the shotgun on the table, and places his backpack on his bed. He looks around at his cabin, at the gay rights posters, then sits at the kitchen table. He thinks about Frankie. About his friends. About those who remained. Many who had already planned their own funerals, but then had to decide what they were going to do with their lives.

They lived for those they lost. Until they could live for themselves again.

This isn't the place for him anymore. He needs to stop being a zombie and start living. He needs to find people—*his* people. While discussing gay sex and love in the 80s, Larry Kramer once said, "The only safe place left is the dark."

It's time to go into the light, or at least fucking try. He gathers up his things again, and heads out.

Quinton pushes the small tip of the blade into Todd's temple, finally ending his misery. Killing that fuck feels like the end of an era, the era of torturing the piece of shit who ruined his year, but also opened him up to so many things.

Like Billy.

Before setting off into the forest, he looks back at the cabin he's spent the last thirty years treading water in. Quinton is unsure of where he's going next or who and what he will find. But he goes anyway.

Into the unknown.
Into the light.

ACKNOWLEDGEMENTS

I want to start by thanking my boyfriend, Aidan. Not only for designing the cover, but also when I look at the quality of my work from the past four years, I see the impact he has had on it. I also want to thank Alvaro Rodriguez, because it was he who convinced me to write this novella and send it in to Ghoulish Books. Since the moment I met Alvaro, he has made me feel like a peer, and someone who deserves to get their work out there. He made me feel like an actual writer and I will always be grateful to him for that. I must also mention Jeff Ching and Scott Hastings. They are some of my oldest friends and are probably the only two people besides me who have read almost everything I've written since age 14 onwards. They continue to inspire me every time I see them and read the crazy-ass shit they come up with.

I would also like to mention Josh Evans, Brandon Kendall, and Dylan Bernbaum for always being willing to read something I've written.

When I began writing this novella, there was a lot of death in my life. I had nightmares thinking about the people I once spent time with now just not existing. I remember them all and always will.

Born in 1987, I never lived through the plague that is written about within these pages, but I always felt it hung over me. A quote that always stuck with me in "The Normal Heart" was Tommy Boatman saying *"We're losing an entire generation. Young men, at the beginning, just gone. Choreographers, playwrights, dancers, actors. All those plays that won't get written now. All those dances, never to be danced.*" It took so many people. Artists who would've been my role models. I wish I could list them all here, but it would sadly be more words than this tiny novella has.

I feel I must acknowledge Larry Kramer. I don't know if there is any other writer that has affected me and my work to the extent that he has. I look at the point where I felt my writing was actually starting to become almost readable, and it was after I read his work. He showed me how to be unapologetically queer and to really use that in my writing instead of shying away from it. I am so grateful I have been able to read his beautiful words.

And finally, my dog Kaufman. I miss you so much, bud.

ABOUT THE AUTHOR

At 16, Warren Wagner realized he was gay at a memorial service for Ronald Reagan and it was all downhill from there. Wagner's screenwriting has placed in multiple contests, most notably as a finalist in the Austin Film Festival screenplay competition. Whether it's comedy, drama, or horror, Wagner's queer perspective makes the material feel fresh and unique. This is his debut novella.

SPOOKY TALES FROM GHOULISH BOOKS 2023

LIKE REAL | Shelly Lyons

ISBN: 978-1-943720-82-8 $16.95

This mind-bending body horror rom-com is a rollicking Cronenbergian gene splice of *Idle Hands* and *How to Lose a Guy in 10 Days*. It's freaky. It's fun. It's LIKE REAL.

XCRMNTMNTN | Andrew Hilbert

ISBN: 978-1-943720-81-1 $14.95

When a pile of shit from space lands near a renowned filmmaker's set, inspiration strikes. Take a journey up a cosmic mountain of excrement with the director and his film crew as they ascend into madness led only by their own vanity and obsession. This is a nightmare about creation. This is a dream about poop. This is a call to arms against vowels. This is *XCRMNTMNTN*.

BOUND IN FLESH | edited by Lor Gislason

ISBN: 978-1-943720-83-5 $16.95

Bound in Flesh: An Anthology of Trans Body Horror brings together 13 trans and non-binary writers, using horror to both explore the darkest depths of the genre and the boundaries of flesh. A disgusting good time for all! Featuring stories by Hailey Piper, Joe Koch, Bitter Karella, and others.

CONJURING THE WITCH | Jessica Leonard

ISBN: 978-1-943720-84-2 $16.95

Conjuring the Witch is a dark, haunted story about what those in power are willing to do to stay in power, and the sins we convince ourselves are forgivable.

WHAT HAPPENED WAS IMPOSSIBLE |
E. F. Schraeder

ISBN: 978-1-943720-85-9 $14.95

Everyone knows the woman who escapes a massacre is a final girl, but who is the final boy? *What Happened Was Impossible* follows the life of Ida Wright, a man who knows how to capitalize on his childhood tragedies . . . even when he caused them.

THE ONLY SAFE PLACE LEFT IS THE DARK|
Warren Wagner
ISBN: 978-1-943720-86-6 $14.95

In *The Only Safe Place Left is the Dark*, an HIV positive gay man must leave the relative safety of his cabin in the woods to brave the zombie apocalypse and find the medication he needs to stay alive.

THE SCREAMING CHILD| Scott Adlerberg
ISBN: 978-1-943720-87-3 $16.95

Scott Adlerberg's *The Screaming Child* is a mystery horror novel told by a grieving woman working on a book about an explorer who was murdered in a remote wilderness region, only to get caught up in a dangerous journey after hearing the distant screams from her own vanished child somewhere in the woods.

RAINBOW FILTH | Tim Meyer
ISBN: 978-1-943720-88-0 $14.95

Rainbow Filth is a weirdo horror novella about a small cult that believes a rare psychedelic substance can physically transport them to another universe.

LET THE WOODS KEEP OUR BODIES| E. M. Roy
ISBN: 978-1-943720-89-7 $16.95

The familiar becomes strange the longer you look at it. Leo Bates navigates a broken sense of reality, shattered memories, and a distrust of herself in order to find her girlfriend Tate and restore balance to their hometown of Eston—if such a thing ever existed to begin with.

SAINT GRIT| Kayli Scholz
ISBN: 978-1-943720-90-3 $14.95

One brooding summer, Nadine Boone pricks herself on a poisonous manchineel tree in the Florida backcountry. Upon self-orgasm, Nadine conjures a witch that she calls Saint Grit. Pitched as *Gummo* meets *The Craft*, Saint Grit grows inside of Nadine over three decades, wreaking repulsive havoc on a suspicious cast of characters in a small town known as Sugar Bends. Comes in Censored or Uncensored cover.

Ghoulish Books
PO Box 1104
Cibolo, TX 78108

☐ LIKE REAL   16.95
☐ XCRMNTMNTN   14.95
☐ BOUND IN FLESH   16.95
☐ CONJURING THE WITCH   16.95
☐ WHAT HAPPENED WAS IMPOSSIBLE   14.95
☐ THE ONLY SAFE PLACE LEFT IS THE DARK   14.95
☐ THE SCREAMING CHILD   16.95
☐ RAINBOW FILTH   14.95
☐ LET THE WOODS KEEP OUR BODIES   16.95
☐ SAINT GRIT   14.95
    Censored | Uncensored

Ship to:

Name   _____

Address _____

City_____State_____Zip _____

Phone Number   _____

                                  Book Total: $_____

                               Shipping Total: $_____

                                 Grand Total: $_____

Not all titles available for immediate shipping. All credit card
purchases must be made online at GhoulishBooks.com. Shipping is
5.80 for one book and an additional dollar for each additional book.
Contact us for international shipping prices. All checks and money
orders should be made payable to Perpetual Motion Machine.

Patreon:
www.patreon.com/pmmpublishing

Website:
www.GhoulishBooks.com

Facebook:
www.facebook.com/GhoulishBooks

Twitter:
@GhoulishBooks

Instagram:
@GhoulishBookstore

Newsletter:
www.PMMPNews.com

Linktree:
linktr.ee/ghoulishbooks

Printed in the USA
CPSIA information can be obtained
at www.ICGtesting.com
LVHW031048181023
761327LV00058B/919